I0691383

THE CARPET
INSTALLER

First Edition

Published by The Nazca Plains Corporation
Las Vegas, Nevada
2010

ISBN: 978-1-935509-18-9

Published by

The Nazca Plains Corporation ®
4640 Paradise Rd, Suite 141
Las Vegas NV 89109-8000

PUBLISHER'S NOTE
The Carpet Installer is a work of fiction created wholly by *Wade
Wright's* imagination. All characters are fictional and any resemblance
to any persons living or deceased is purely by accident. No portion
of this book reflects any real person or events.

Cover,
Andrei Vishnyakov and Kirill Kurashov

Art Director,
Blake Stephens

DEDICATION

To each and every working person that improves not only his or her personal life, but also that of many, many more untold individuals.

THE CARPET INSTALLER

First Edition

Wade Wright

CONTENTS

CHAPTER ONE:

Measuring Everything

David, a single gay guy, 34 years old, had purchased the house about one year earlier, and the time had finally come for him to – finally, get rid of the terrible old 1960's shag carpet, that completely filled the house.

The bathroom had been re-done, the kitchen was finally finished, and the last remaining inside project was the terrible orange carpet that he had hated so badly ever since he bought the house.

David had done his fair share of "shopping around" to find exactly what he wanted, and at price that he felt comfortable with.

The day had come for the installation crew to come and do the final measurements so that the correct amount of carpet was ordered. Yeah – special order – not just some old carpet that was already in stock. David had decided that after living with that damn orange shag carpet, the kind that you actually combed, he wanted to have something that was very unusual from the norm.

The doorbell rang and David then asked his friend Joe, that was on the phone, to hold on for a moment, that he would be right back, and David quickly answered the door.

Two installation men were at the door. David let them in, and quickly told them, "All of the three bedrooms, the hall, the family room and the living room. OK guys? I've got a guy on the phone, so unless you need me for something, I'll get back to him. OK?"

"Yeah right. No problem," the lead man replied. "All we need to do is measure, and then we will be out of here."

"OK Thanks!" David answered and returned to Joe on the phone. The phone conversation continued, and the installation men made their way through the house, doing their measuring.

As the men finished, David and Joe were still talking. The lead installation man came into the den where David was at, and told him that they were done, but needed to know some information about getting the installation all set up.

"The carpet will be here in one week, one week from today. When we install, will your wife or somebody be here so that we can come in and maybe do it on Thursday?"

"Well, I'm single," David answered. "So I guess I will have to be the one that is home when you are ready."

"Oh, there's nobody else that just might happen to be here so we don't have to bother you during the business day?" The installer inquired.

"Uhhh – no, it's just me, so I guess we'll just have to schedule it when I am here. Or I'll just plan on taking a day off whenever you guys are ready."

"Oh, OK then." The installer replied. "Uhhhh, say – how about, then, if I stop by here Monday or Tuesday night after work to see what schedule works best for you then. OK? I'll just stop by, by myself, if that is OK with you, and then we can decide when to do the work? OK?"

David very confusingly replied, "Well, yeah – I guess if that is what you want to do."

"Yeah, I'll do that. You aren't going to be busy then on, let's say Monday night then, is that right?"

David was getting really confused, but did answer, "No, I won't be busy, I'll be here."

"OK, I'll be here at 7:00 Monday night then. OK?"

"Yeah – OK." David answered, but rather bewildered as to just what this whole thing was all about.

"Wouldn't you rather just give me a phone call instead of driving all the way out here?" David asked.

"No! No! I'd really rather stop by if I might. It will just be me! I won't stay too long, but I think it would work better if I came out. We like to really take care of our customers in kind of a first class way. OK?"

David finally said, "OK! I'll see you then."

The installer guy went on out to the truck where his helper had been waiting for him, and David returned to his conversation with Joe on the phone.

"Joe, did you hear all of that while I was talking to him? I have no idea of what in the hell that was all about. Why in the hell does he need to come here to do the scheduling. Hell man, we could have decided right now when to do it since he knows for sure when the carpet will be in. Man I am really confused of what in the hell that is all about."

David and Joe both decided that neither one of them could figure out just what in the hell that was all about, but if that is the way the guy wanted to do it, then that's what David would do. He told Joe, "Shit man, I really can't figure that one out. I'll talk to you later and let you know how it all comes out. All I can say right now is that I sure in the hell, hope that carpet is in when it is supposed to be. I'll talk to you later, man. Bye."

David finally finished his conversation, hung up the phone and headed down the hall to the bathroom, for obvious purposes.

As he walked past the bedroom door, he almost yelled out – "Oh shit man! Oh shit!"

He immediately ran back to the phone and called Joe.

"Joe, it's David! Joe, my God, Joe! I think I know why that guy was so set on coming out here. He kept saying things about how he would be all by himself, and you know he asked me about my wife being here and all that shit, man? I have two dildos laying out on the bed stand. I forgot they were out there. Joe, he saw them!! He is all hot and bothered about those dildos, I bet!"

"Oh shit!" Joe replied. "David, what did that guy look like? Can you describe him? I bet he wants to come back and play with you! He saw those dildos and then he went though all those questions about the wife and all that stuff, he knows you are gay! I think he wants to come back and play!"

"Oh shit, Joe, what do I do?"

"What did the guy look like? Is he somebody that you might want to play with?"

"Oh shit, man – I don't remember looking him over that much. I was busy. Oh shit, man, I don't know! There were two of them. He was the older guy. I'd say he was probably in his early thirty's. Not bad looking – I mean I didn't want to throw up when I answered the door. He had a uniform outfit on, so I couldn't really tell about his body too much, but hell man, I did not know there was going to be a quiz later about him. Shit, Joe, do you really think that is why he insisted on coming back out here?"

"Speaking straight forward – hell yes I do! He asked too many funny personal questions that he really did not need to know. He was probably making sure you did not use those dildos on your wife, and he now knows you do not have a wife. He also knows you live there alone, so he now also knows that those dildos are yours. He has you figured out, and he intends to play with you. What night is he coming back, Monday?"

"Yeah, Joe, Monday. Oh shit Joe, what in the hell do I do when he gets here. How do I act. What do I do? Act like nothing happened? Shit Joe, his helper must have seen them too. Hell man, both of those guys saw my dildos lying out there. You know Joe, now I do remember hearing him tell the other guy to go to the truck, and that he would be out in a minute. He did kind of chase that other guy out before he started asking all those questions."

"Well, why were they out on your bed stand, anyway?" Joe asked, rather inquisitively.

"They just kind of got used last night, and I just forgot to put them away after I washed them this morning. We got up a little later than we intended to, and so I got a little confused in getting everything done and helping him get out of here. No, no. Nobody that you know.

Well, I don't think so anyway. He is a damn good top, so since you know every top in the county, maybe you do know him. No – all I know is that his first name is Steve, and no I did not get around to asking him his last name. So I will find out later – OK? Hey man. Last night my mind was not exactly on what the guy's name was – OK? I had more fun things on my mind, and stuck up in my ass than to worry about names!"

"Well, I guess about all I can say right now is, thank goodness you did have the presence of mind to at least wash them. Can you tell by the way they are laying on the table, did the carpet guys move them any? Are they just like the way you laid them down?"

"I don't think they were moved any, but when I saw them laying there I kind of freaked out and ran back here to call you. Hey man, what in the hell do I do now?"

"Hey David, I'd say maybe you have a playmate on the leash, if you want to go for it. From everything you told me about what this guy said and asked, I'd say he's all game. I guess now it's just wait until Monday night! Right?"

"Yeah, Joe, I guess you are right! OK man. I'll figure out what to do before Monday evening, I guess. Hey, maybe after I see him again, then I will decide if I want to do anything or not. Hell, I just might make him let me know, that he saw them, before I do anything. At least that way I will be able to see just how anxious he is for fooling around, can't I?"

"Hey all I can say right now is, why you? Why not me? Nothing exciting like this ever happens to me? I need some fun too, you know!"

"Hey man, the only reason nothing like this ever happens to you is because you are sharp enough to put your sex toys away before some guys come into your house and sees 'em. Hey Joe, I'll talk to you later man! I got to try an' figure out how I'm going to handle this. Bye!" David hung up the phone, and rather started pondering his next move, as far as his Monday night visitor was concerned.

The rest of David's Wednesday went by, as did Thursday, Friday, Saturday, Sunday and it was now Monday! The Monday that

David had been anxiously, kind of, looking forward to, but at the same time rather worried about not really knowing if things really were as he had decided, or maybe totally different than he has assumed.

The house had been fully inspected this time. David made sure no tail-tell items had been left lying around. Since the dildos had been out and used again, the night before, he had made sure to re-store them in their correct hiding space immediately after they had been cleaned.

His, now favorite 'top man', Steve, had visited again Sunday night and David had asked Steve to please make sure he, David, did not leave the toys out in plan view again. Steve found David's description of the carpet man's return quite interesting and fully informed David that he wanted a full and detailed accounting of whatever happened after the carpet man arrived, and before he left!

Seven o'clock on the button, and the front door bell rang.

David quickly looked himself over in the hall mirror to see if he was making a proper appearance. Not that he could do anything about it at this time, since the man was now on the porch waiting for him to open the door.

David's anxiety over the past four or five days had gotten him mentally, completely in the mood for whatever exciting things just might happen, even though he did have to admit that he really could not remember just what this man looked like. Nor, even how he was built. Right now, David was hoping that his slight memories of this man had not been up-graded just due to his excitement of thinking maybe, maybe, something was in store, and his questions of just how this was all going to come to the surface, so that things could happen, if they could and should!

The original "casual" business attire that David did originally have on – he had decided was way too stuffy. Way too stuffy if he wanted to make any type of a "fun person" appearance to this man of "mystery."

After making three or four decisions about his attire, he had finally decided that a neatly pressed pair of Levi cutoffs and a simple white T-shirt with gym shoes would look very appropriate for a man that was just simply home for the evening. Not dressy, not too way-out sexy, but yet just leveled to the point that cutoffs are advisable for showing off some very nice muscular calves. And of course, the T-shirt is such a standard piece of apparel, very widely accepted in almost all environments, but thankfully it did manage to offer a very nice presentation of a young man's rather strong muscular upper body and the biceps that bulged and hung to the side of the shirt.

David yelled, "Coming!" And then reached for the door and opened it, to, once again, get a more conscious look at this man that he had mentally played with for the entire last four or five days.

"Hello! How you doing?" The visitor asked as David opened the door and for a slight moment, a slightly little too long of a moment, simply stood there and let his mouth hang open.

"Hey, I'm doing great! How about you? Come on in!"

David invited the, "carpet man" in, as he had recently been referring to him, as he had told his friends about the funny little visit he was expecting and the reasons behind it. As he did, he realized that if this was the same man as the one there last Wednesday, he certainly did improve his appearance by dumping the baggy uniform clothes that David was sure he had on last Wednesday. David did admit, that he had not really paid too much attention to the man last week, but now he was certain that it had to all be due to his rather, un-flattery attire on that day.

As David extended his hand for a hand shake, he did muster enough courage to ask, "Uh, you are the same guy that was here last Wednesday, right?"

"Yeah, I am! I'm Todd. I'm the same guy. Why? Am I hard to recognize out of the crappie uniforms they give us? Got to admit – just as soon as I can, I dump that stuff and put some of my own clothes on after work. I guess when they ordered uniforms for me, somebody must have thought I weighed in at about 50 pounds heavier."

"Yeah, I guess so!" David replied with a smile. A rather broad smile! "I'm sorry, but yeah, I do admit that I really did not pay to much attention to you or what you looked like last Wednesday, but if I had been told to go find you someplace, I do admit that I would never have picked you out of a crowd, as the same guy. Yeah, I guess maybe they don't have the best uniforms for you, do they? Anyway, sorry, I just needed to make sure I was talking to the same guy!"

Todd's present attire was much more becoming to him, and his 29 year old body. The body of an obvious former athlete, or perhaps still a current one, since everything was certainly looking very fit and proper to David!

As the two men entered the living room, with David in the rear and definitely checking out the ass on this guy, Todd started to explain, "Mr. Stanley, we did get confirmation today that the carpet will be here Wednesday."

"Uhh, wait Todd. Please don't refer to me as Mr. Stanley. As I've always said, only the undertaker and the tax man can refer to me as Mr. Stanley. I'm not that damn primp and proper! Just please call me David! Don't make me feel uncomfortable with all the formal customer approach crap. Let's just be friends. I mean, after all, the day you guys lay it, we will be spending most of the day together anyway, so let's just be Todd and David, OK?"

As David expressed the statement, "the day you guys lay it," made his mind wonder just slightly as he then remembered that ass he had just checked out and was wishing he could "lay it!"

"Thanks! Thanks! I do appreciate that a lot! You know we service people do have to maintain our respect for our customers, but when somebody like you lets us take the guard down, it sure does help a lot. I appreciate that a lot! Like I was saying, we got confirmation that the carpet will be here Wednesday. Is Thursday workable for you?"

"Yeah. Yeah, Thursday is OK. I can sign up for a personal day, for that day so that I can be home all day, so yeah, that's OK. What time will you guys be here?"

"If 8:00 is OK with you, we can be here at that time."

"Yeah 8:00 is great! How long will it probably take? All day?"

"For this size of installation, we will plan on all day. May not take that long, but if not, then we'll be out of here earlier."

"OK, whatever."

"Uh, there is one thing that I do need to kind of discuss with you first though."

"OK? Yeah?"

"Well, I'll have the guy with me that was here last week, Jimmy, and I'll also have a couple more younger guys to help move the furniture in and out. What I need to talk to you about is – well – this is kind of maybe a little touchy – but hey, we are both men and I don't think I'll offend you any if I mention it."

With anxiety in his heart, just hoping the right subject is about to be approached, David asked, "Yeah?"

"Well, last week when Jimmy and I were here, I saw some dildos on your night stand. I don't know if you kind of always let them lay around or not, but can I ask if maybe you don't have them out and showing? Poor Jimmy, he's already about to climb the fence in asking everything about what he saw, and I'm not so sure I've got all the answers for him, and I know damn well that if those other two see something like that, I've got big problems on my hands."

"Oh my God Todd, I'm sorry! Right after you guys left, I went past the bedroom and saw them laying there and I almost freaked out myself. I'm sorry! All that stuff will be well hidden. Don't need to worry about it happening again! I got a little careless and I'm sorry. So this Jimmy. What's he asking? Did they really freak him out or something?"

"Hey, David, can I get real honest with you?"

"Yeah sure, of course. I'm more the one that asked the questions. I'm not sure if they freaked him out more, or maybe me! I have a dildo at home that I use on my girlfriend, but it sure as hell is not the size of either one of those! I've never been around anybody that I knew that owned one that big. Do you mind if I get real blunt with you, and ask if you use that whole thing?"

David sat there realizing that the, wished for, highly anticipated, conversation that he had dreamt about maybe happening for the past four or five days, was actually now in progress! He shyly replied, "Well, yeah. Yeah I do. You do know I'm a gay guy, right?"

"Oh yeah, I know that! You kind of told me that last week when you told me you were single and no wife. When you told me that, and I had already seen those dildos, in there, I kind of pretty quickly put two and two together. That's why I wanted to come back here tonight, if possible. I wanted to just get gutsy and up-front and ask you about them. See, Julie, my girlfriend, and I have looked at some like that in the toy store, and we've always wondered just who, and how they use them. Is this alright if we talk this stuff? I'm really curious, and I feel like maybe you and I are enough alike, well except that you are gay and I'm straight, but anyway, enough alike to talk about this stuff. Is it OK? Can you tell me how those big ones are used?"

"Well, I've got to admit, that I've never really had anybody just come right out and ask stuff like this before, but hey – like you say, we are enough alike that I guess it's not too off base to discuss this stuff. You've got the guts to ask, I should have the guts to answer."

"Wow! Thanks! I've got to admit that I really did feel like I was putting my neck out on the line doing this, but I just knew you were the kind of a guy I could ask this stuff about and not have you get all mad. That's why I never talk this stuff over with any of my straight buddies. I tried once, but hell, all I got was a lot of crap from them all trying to act like they knew what in the hell they were talking about, when I don't think one of them had any idea of what in the world he was saying. I can talk to gay guys a whole lot easier about sex stuff than I can the straight guys."

"Well, thanks! I consider that a complement! But, I've got to remind you that I am a gay guy, and for me to sit here and talk about using dildos, either on me, or on someone else, it's a little different for me than for you. I'll be talking and remembering what two gay guys do together, and let's face it – you are not some slob! I know since you are straight, maybe talking about some outrageous sex actions with a guy is not a turn on for you, but sitting here talking about asses and dildos and looking at you sitting there, all hot as hell, in your tight Levi's, well that is something else. I'll try, but, I've got to admit, I'm getting all hot and bothered inside already! Us gay guys get hot for sex just as quickly as you straight guys do! It's just with us, it's for sex with some hot hunky guy, wearing hot, tight hugging, Levi's like you are wearing, instead of with some gal that runs around with almost nothing on. I do hope you are smart enough to realize that gay guys like to make it with hot looking guys, and when the subject is sex, you've got to expect the gay guy to get all hot and bothered just like a straight guy does! Especially if he's talking to some hot looking guy! Yeah, I'll talk about this stuff, and tell you how to use those dildos, but if you see me eyeballing you and probably specifically your crotch, you better expect it! You don't look like you did the other day with that messy uniform outfit on. You know what? Tonight any gay guy would get hot over you, even if not talking sex!"

As Todd listened to David talk about how gay guys get all hot and bothered too, he reached down, rubbed his crotch slightly and looking directly at David said, "I've never made it with a guy before. Are you saying that maybe I'm hot enough looking to you, that maybe you would like to have sex with me? Is that what you are saying?"

"Oh shit man! You need to ask that question? Is this all a come on, or are you suggesting that you want us to do something? What's up here? Let's not be playing games!"

"David, I have never been so damn straight forward in doing something or asking for something than I am now. These last few days, after I got so damn cock sure of myself when I told you I needed to come over here to set up the installation, I have been shaking in my shoes wondering if I would actually have the nerve to tell you why I was really here. When I saw those dildos lying there, I decided that I wanted you to show me how to use one of those big dildos. Julie has been wanting to get one, so she can do my ass with it, and I need to know if I can take something like that up in my ass first. Can we, maybe, see if I can take something like that up in my ass?"

CHAPTER TWO:

The Bathhouse Installation

"Todd, I've got to admit, I sure as hell have never had some guy be quite as up-front on something like this, as you are! I've got to admit you've got guts, man. I know when I was younger and wondering about gay stuff I sure as the hell never had the guts to just tell some guy that I wanted to see if I could get some big dildo, or anything else for that matter, stuck up in my ass."

"Hey David, don't make this rough for me please! Like I told you man, I've been shaking in my shoes ever since I lied to you and told you I needed to come back to schedule the installation. I've never been this gutsy with anything before, so I guess I really did want to at least talk to you about trying this, even if you said no. Please don't make me think I did the wrong thing – please!"

"You've never done any gay stuff at all? You told me earlier that you've never done anything with a guy before – is that right?"

"Yeah, it's right. There was once, about a year ago, that I almost did, well, I guess would have, but then things did not work out right, and I never got the chance again, or maybe never got the nerve again."

"What happened about a year ago when it almost happened, and then things did not work out right? What happened then?"

"Well, you guys have a – what do you call it – a bathhouse, down on South Brooker Street, right?"

"Yeah, there's a bathhouse down there. Not mine, but yeah, there's one down there."

"Yeah, I didn't mean it was yours, I meant you gay guys have a bathhouse there. Right?"

"Yeah, there is. What about it?"

"Well, about a year ago our company, the carpet company, sold them some carpet and I helped install it. When the owners of the bathhouse ordered it, they explained to my boss about where it was for and what the place was like and told my boss that they did want a professional installation so that it was done right, and did he have installers that could work in that kind of a place for a day without having problems with where they were at and who they would be around. Mr. Stenner told them that he would get together a special team to use and that he knew it would not be a problem. He told them that for the size of their order, he would go out of his way getting the right guys together. Well, anyway, for about a week he kind of kept asking me things like, 'Hey, if you found out that you were doing an installation for a gay guy, would that bother you any?' Or maybe he'd ask me if I had any gay friends. Or stuff like that. I was starting to think maybe he thought I was gay."

"Well, it does kind of sound like he was checking you out, doesn't it?"

"Yeah, I sure thought so. Anyway, on that next Monday night just as I was getting ready to head home, he told me he needed to talk to me. He told me about the guys buying the carpet, and how he was putting together a special crew of guys to install it. I was the only one from our company that he was using. He did not think the other guys – they were all married and older guys, would be so agreeable to do it, so he had found three more guys that he trusted, and their companies had said he could hire them for a day, and he wanted to know if I was interested in make some pretty good extra money that coming Sunday, by helping install at the bathhouse. Hey, it was more than twice my normal pay, so of course I said yes! Mr. Stenner told me to keep my mouth shut about it since I was the only one from the company that he was using, and the carpet was being delivered directly to the bathhouse early that Sunday morning. He did not particularly want this situation to be a topic of discussion around the company. So anyway, it was all done kind of secret, like."

"So, you're one of the guys that installed that new Royal Blue carpet a year ago? You helped do that?"

"Yeah, I did. Yeah, I helped. I was one of the guys there that day!"

"Well, shit man! What a deal! How weird! You a straight guy, installing carpet in a gay bathhouse! How did that go?"

"All of us were straight guys! But we all new what the deal was before we agreed to do it. We were told the bathhouse was not going to be closed, but that the members would be told what was going on that day, and to respect us since we were there to work."

"You're kidding! I heard after it was installed it was definitely a different day around there that day. What happened?"

"When we got there they had a sign up telling the members about the installation. Part of it was pretty funny. Like one thing on it said something like, 'If a man is found on his hands and knees, remember he is installing the new carpet, he's not waiting for one of you guys to mount him!' Another part of the sign told them to have at least gym shorts on while around us, and another told them that when we were laying the hallway carpet, that they had to go around the other way and not try stepping over us.' I really think whoever wrote that sign had a pretty good sense of humor. I found part of it funny."

"Yeah, I heard that was a pretty fun day there that day, too. I'm damn sorry I wasn't there. So, how and what happened?"

Well, the bathhouse guy, owner I guess, had already told us that they would give each of us a lock and a locker if we wanted to bring anything with us, like snacks or maybe gym clothes if any of us actually wanted to maybe hit the hot tub or the weight room before we left. I took swim trunks and of course some snacks to munch on once in awhile. We did not need to take lunch. They, the bathhouse guys, ordered and paid for lunch for us! And it was not just sandwiches!

It was full big meals, from the dining room of the Hillway Hotel! I mean man, they treated us nice! I had steak that day for lunch. And then I also had pork chops for supper. We ate good that day!"

"Well, shit! Now I know where my membership money goes to! Feeding the straight guys! Oh well. Better that, than a lot of places it could be going to! So – you told me that you almost did something once, and then this bathhouse thing came up. Associated, I guess?"

"Yeah, yeah they are. I'm sorry, just trying to explain how everything happened."

"We were working in there, laying the carpet, and some of the members would come by and see how we were doing and of course make comments and just have some fun. The day really was kind of fun. Some of the guys would kind of "accidentally" drop their towels while walking past someplace where we could see them. Some of them had some pretty big hardons too! We were there all day since we had the whole lounge area place, the hallways, the offices and I guess it is some kind of a meeting room. Well, anyway, about 2:00 in the afternoon I saw some really nice looking, very nicely attired tall black man come in with his gym bag in his hand. He had to go around where this Tim guy and I were working. He nodded at me as he went by and I just kind of nodded back. I did think he was pretty nice looking and from the way he looked as he walked by, I thought maybe he was probably pretty well built, too."

"Did you have on your baggy uniform pants like you did out here last week?"

"No, no! I forgot to mention that Mr. Stenner asked me to not wear my uniform pants since this was going to be kind of a different deal, and he told me to just wear something that I was comfortable working in. Hey – cut offs man – cutoffs! I think that should be the uniform all of the time anyway, so I was more than glad to just wear my own clothes."

"What did you have on for a shirt?"

"Oh, at the time that black man came in, I didn't have a shirt on. Right after we had lunch, some of the guys there in the club starting goofing around with me and this Tim guy, and they bet us we wouldn't take our shirts off and work without shirts, and after one guy offered me a ten, and then another said he'd match it, I decided hell, for twenty bucks, I'll work without a shirt."

"Did that Tim guy take his off?"

"No, nobody offered him any money, so it ended up just being me."

"Well, if you had cutoffs on and no shirt, I sure as hell can understand why the tall black man nodded at you! He had eyes on you young man!"

"Yeah, I know! Well, yeah I kind of guess maybe he did. He kept coming around wherever I was at and he'd stop and talk a little and then he'd move on. He just had a towel wrapped around himself most of the time, and oh man – he was well built, damn well built! But then later he came by, when I was working kind of by myself in that conference room, or whatever it is, and he had a real, real tight pair of very short, white shorts on. Not the street type, well maybe if on some smaller guy, but on him, the material was stretched tight, real, real tight! Those shorts were so damn tight on him, I really wondered if he had borrowed them from some smaller guy, just so that he would have some really tight, hugging, shorts on. Man, they looked good, but I'm not so sure he could have worn them out on the street though! That was the first time that I ever looked at a man, or some part of a man and wanted to reach out and touch him. He was showing me a hardon that he had laying sideways across his leg. That damn thing was at least nine or ten inches long. Damn man, I had never seen one that damn big, even in some sex magazines that I've looked at. Oh shit, he was making me wanna feel it! I had never ever felt that way about a man or a guy's body before, but David, that day I really did want to see what his dick felt like! I was on the floor on my hands and knees working on that carpet, and he just stood there right in front of my face! My eyes and his dick were right at the same height. I just sat there and stared at it! He never moved! He just stood there, and I think he was wanting me to reach for it! And I wanted too! I knew I couldn't, but man, oh how I wanted to feel it! He knew damn well that I was almost in shock looking at it. He kept watching my eyes when I was looking at it. I think he really knew I wanted to feel it! I know he had to have jerked on it before he came in there where I was at, cause it was so hard! He had a major hardon standing there right in front of my face! Man that damn thing was big!"

"So, what in the hell happened? Did you feel it or anything?"

"No, hell no! I never got to! I think, no – hell no, – I know I was really, really wanting to though! He kept making comments about how there were some rooms available if I could take a break, and it was all in fun, but I know that if I had dropped my tools and stood up and followed him, he would have taken me into one of those rooms. Oh, ever since that day, I've wished I could have gone in there with him. I really do! I've always wondered just what would have happened if I had gone in there with him. I've always tried to maybe just imagine what I could have done or learned that day! I wanted to go follow him so badly that day! I think he is one of the reasons why I finally got up enough nerve to be here tonight! Ever since that day, man, I've wished I would have pulled those tight white trunks off of him and let that great big rod he was showing me, come flying out! I really know now, how much I really wanted to feel his dick! I wish now that I had grabbed it! Man, I do! His dick was just about as big as that biggest dildo you had laying in there the other day! When I saw that dildo, all I could think about was that guy and his great big dick that he was showing me! That's when I decided that I was going to tell you that I needed to come back out here. If Jimmy hadn't been with me that day, I would have told you then that I wanted you to teach me some stuff! I was really sorry he was with me!"

"Well, maybe it's working out better this way! Ever since I found out that I had left those dildos laying out, I've been hoping something like this was going to happen when you got here, but all I could do was maybe hope, since I couldn't even really remember much of what you were like. I sure as hell did not remember you being this damn hot! You are hot, guy, you are hot!"

"Thanks man! I feel better now, knowing you think that! I do! I really do!"

"What happened then with you and the black guy? Did he just leave then or what happened."

"Hey, that job took us until almost midnight to get finished and of course he had to leave way before that. When he left that room where he was standing there right in front of my face, he reached down once and grabbed hold of his dick, but even though he pulled it out in front some, those shorts were so damn tight on him that he really couldn't pull it out very much! When he did that, he looked at me, right in the face, and put a great big smile on his face, and then he licked his lips. David, I know damn well he knew he was getting me all flustered and shook! Later, he came in where I was at after he got all nicely re-dressed, and he just handed me his business card, smiled, turned and walked away. He didn't say anything. He just smiled at me when he handed that to me. I couldn't do anything but stand there and kind of wish things had been different. I really, really didn't want to see him go. I watched him walk away as long as I could see him before he had to turn a corner."

"Well, the card! What about the card? Where's the card!?"

"Oh, I still have it. I've never had the guts to call him, but I've kept the card hidden at home."

"Hidden!? Hidden, you mean from your girl friend?"

"Yeah."

"What else do you have hidden from her, besides that card?"

"Oh just some magazines that have some pictures of some hot guys in them, and a friend gave me a brochure once of some bondage stuff, that I kind of like looking at, and kind of thinking about being used on me sometime, and once I got hold of one of the local gay papers that have all the bar addresses in it, so I kept it. That's all. Just that stuff!"

"Well, why in the hell haven't you ever called this black man? Obviously he wanted you to call or he would not have given you his card! Shit man, from what you have described to me, if you aren't going to call him, give me that card! I sure as the hell will!"

"Oh, I've wanted to so many times, but every time I get the card out, I freak out and just can't dial it! I don't know! I know I've wanted to, but I guess maybe I'm afraid that I might have misunderstood that guy that day at the bathhouse. Maybe he really is not interested in me. Hell, it's been so long now that he probably wouldn't even know who I am!"

"Hey! The man gave you his card! How could you have misunderstood him and what he wanted? He stood there right in front of your face with his raging hardon, and then before he walked away, he tugged on it, once again right in front of your face, and then he licked his lips! How could anybody misunderstand that? He was really hot for you and he was hoping you would actually go to one of the rooms with him! He has no way of contacting you! He wanted you to call him! Call him, and when he answers the phone just remind him that you are the carpet installer. I am damn sure he will immediately remember. Now you do still have his card, right?"

"Yeah, I do! You really think he will know who I am?"

"Hell yes man! First place – if you were working in there that day with no shirt on, I know damn well he will remember you. Right now you are standing there, well – leaning there, with a shirt on, and I can't see everything that I'm wanting to see, although I do intend to see it all very shortly, and I can tell you man, you are one hot dude dressed, so I can imagine just how excited that guy got if he walked in and found you in there with no shirt on! Come on – pull that shirt off, let me see what the big black man got to lust over that day! Show me what you've got man!"

Todd stood up from leaning back on the kitchen counter, which he and David had found as a rather convenient conversation space, and he pulled his polo pullover up and off of his head.

"Oh shit man! No wonder that man wanted you in a room! Wow, what a fucking hot chest, man! OK – now the rest! You came out here tonight to find out about dildos, and I'm sure you already know, you're sure not going to find out anything with Levi's on. Give Daddy the whole show!"

Standing there in the kitchen, now without a shirt on, but otherwise fully dressed, Todd took a deep breath as he heard his host instruct him to finish taking everything else off."

"Oh shit man, this is making me so fucking nervous, man! It is!"

"Hey, I know that, and I like that! I kind of know what you are feeling right now, and I am enjoying watching you go through it. I know you are nervous as hell right now, standing there, in my kitchen, in front of me, and being told to strip it all off and present yourself completely naked to another man. I know you are nervous as hell right now. This is something that you have never done. Hell, not even in a doctor's office. When he wants you to strip, he hands you some little hospital gown that hardly covers your butt, but then he leaves the room while you get everything off and get re-covered again. Hey man – not this time! This time the man gets to stand right here and watch you take everything off, one item at a time! I get to watch you go back to just like you were when you were born! Naked! Totally naked and presenting your completely bare assed body, to some other guy, for him to look at and touch, and that being some guy that you hardly even know! Right? I know you are nervous! I want you to be nervous! You are going to remember this night for the rest of your life, and I want it to be a night well worth remembering! I want you to remember how damn nervous you were the first time you were giving yourself to another guy and the first time you were finally feeling some other guy's ass and his dick. Remember, guys only get one time, for it to be their first time, and the more nervous and exciting it is, the better it is! Not only tonight, but every time you look back at it."

"Oh, I know you're right! You are so right! I knew it could probably be kind of a stupid for me to do something like this, but man, I've been wanting to do something with a guy for so long now, that I just decided that I had to do whatever it takes to get a chance. David – I've got to admit that the way you are giving me instructions, is really a turn on to me! It's letting me know I'm with a real man. One that can take charge and bark orders! I like that! Oh shit, I am so fucking nervous and excited – but the way you're making me do stuff, that's telling me that I did do the right thing by coming over here and telling you I wanted you to show me some stuff. I knew nobody was ever going to come to me and just make me do the things you are now making me do! Oh, I've been trying to find somebody like you for a long time now, and thank goodness I guess those dildos were my signal that I finally found someone."

As David spread a broad smile across his face, he asked. "Well, I guess maybe it's going to be more than just dildos tonight, right?"

"Oh yeah, if we can! Please, please, I need to do this! I really do!"

"Well, good! I'm damn glad now that I left those dildos out!"

"Now, let's see the goods here man. Kick those shoes off and get those Levi's off so I can take a good close-up look at your manhood! I can tell already it's standing at attention, so I guess you are real ready to let me take a good, close-up inspection of it – right? No other guy has ever played with it, right?"

"Oh no, no! No guy has ever done anything with my dick, or even touched it! Oh shit man, I am fucking nervous and feel like I'm about to pass out! Oh shit man! I never expected to be this damn nervous about letting some guy look at my dick and know you are going to grab hold of it! Of shit man, I'm getting real horny man! I'm getting really horny! God man, this is more exciting than the first time I fucked a gal! Oh God! Are you gonna suck on me tonight, too?"

The sight of David standing there still full clothed and Todd now almost completely naked, but with a major bulge showing in the front of his Levi's, would have been a great photo shot for any gay magazine. David was now in complete control, and Todd's statement of how he was so glad David was giving him straight forward instructions, just gave David that much more authority in his voice, as he told Todd just what he was to do. David knew that Todd was now at his mercy.

As Todd kicked his shoes off, unbuckled his belt, and un-fastened the top button on his Levi's, David stood there and thanked God that for once in his life, doing some stupid mistake like leaving two dildos out in the open was really paying back, big time!

David gasped as Todd dropped his Levi's to his knees and his seven inch long, and almost two inch wide, uncut sausage meat stood at military attention for a complete "company" inspection! Todd was not wearing any briefs, and when the Levi's went down, the dick came flying out!

"Holly shit man! My God, look at how God damn thick that rod of yours is! Oh my God! What a fucking rod you've got! Oh my God yes! Hell yes, I will be sucking on you tonight! Hell yes, I will be! My God I wonder how much of that I can get in my mouth! Man I feel my throat getting choked up already! Shit man! I had no idea you were hung like that! Hell man, if I had known that earlier we sure as the hell would not have been standing here in the kitchen talking this long! Todd, do you fuck gals with that thing?"

Todd looked at David and rather shyly, answered, "Yeah. Yeah, but some of 'em make me go real slow. Well, yeah I kind of guess they all do except for one gal that I fucked up in New York City once, and I really don't know what all she was into. I know she kept begging for more and more, and she kept yelling for faster and faster! I fucked her as hard and as fast as I could, but it never was enough! She is the only one that I ever got to fuck that way, and I've read some stuff where guys like to get fucked real hard and fast with a big dick up their ass. That's one of the reasons why I want to see what fucking a guy is like and what getting fucked in the butt is like. I want to find me some guy that will let me fuck him good and hard, like I did that gal up in New York that time. And maybe that's the way I'll want to get fucked once I find out what it's like! Seriously, that's one of the reasons that Julie wants to get a big dildo and use it on me. She says she wants me to see what getting something big and thick rammed up in me real fast, feels like. She won't let me fuck her that way. I tried a couple of times and she made me quit. She thinks that if she rams my ass with a big dildo then I will quit trying to fuck her fast and hard. What I really want is to find me some guy that really likes it up in his ass like that, so I can just fuck the hell out of him and have him ask for more! Julie's so sure I won't like it when it happens to me, but from some of the stuff I've read, I think I might like it!"

"You know, you might. You just might! Some guys like it rougher than they can usually find it, and you just might be one of those guys!"

"You know I told you about that bondage stuff, I have that brochure of. That stuff turns me on too! I want somebody to use that stuff on me some time! David, I really think I'm probably one of those guys that likes it up the ass good and rough. Maybe I just like sex too rough to have sex with a gal! Maybe I really need to just have sex with guys so that I can get really rough and get treated back real rough! I've really got to find out if I'm one of those guys! I've got to find out if I'm really like some wild animal and the rougher it is the better it is."

"You know, you just might be – and if so – that's OK! Everybody does not have to be the same, nor do everything the same!"

"I'm really tired of just jerking it off when I want some fast rough sex. Is what I've read right? Do some guys like a big cock rammed up in their ass as hard as they can get it? Is that for real? Do some guys really like that? David, I want to find me some guy that I can fuck really hard enough that it wears me out, before he tells me to stop. And maybe he can be the same guy that fucks me and my ass as hard as I can take it! Are there guys like that? I haven't even been fucked yet and David I already know I want it rough! Can you do that for me tonight? Can you get real rough with me tonight so I can see if that's the way I am?"

CHAPTER THREE:

Oh My Day is Finally Here!

"Man there is no way in hell that I thought that I'd be getting together tonight with something as hot as you are man! Todd, you are one damn hot man! Tell you what. I think maybe the best way for us to get started is for you to kind of be the aggressive one, and you completely undress me. Let's let you kind of be the aggressor, and I will just kind of play as if you are taking advantage of me. Come on man, reach over here and pull my shirt off. Yeah, pull, yeah – doing good! Take all my clothes off of me Todd!"

David was really playing the very innocent one, and although maybe Todd was not so aware of it, having Todd undress him was becoming a complete and total turn on to David.

"Yeah, now slide your hands down along my chest, feel my tits, and feel my chest. Yeah, feel me and kind of get used to feeling my skin. Yeah, man, slide your hands up and around my back. Hug me! Yeah, pull me toward you man, yeah kind of pull me and hug me. Feel my bare skin against your bare skin! You know, you are the man here that wants to do some stuff, so you play with me and get me all ready to be used by you and that fucking big dick you've got there! Yeah, play with my body! You're the man, play with your boy! Do things to me man, yeah – do things that you've been wanting to do, to some guy!"

Completely unaware of exactly what was really happening, David's technique of having Todd play the dominate roll, was really working out very well. I was working out very well for Todd! He was getting hot with just feeling David's skin and feeling his own bare body up against David's skin, even though he had not yet taken David's cutoffs, off. At the same time, instructing and having Todd handle him in this fashion, was definitely getting David very hot and very bothered! His juices were definitely starting to flow! He was now playing with a man that had never been played with before, and a man that was wanting him to do stuff and he was asking for it, and David was more than ready to deliver!

"Yeah, undo my cutoffs and let them slide down! Yeah man, get me out of these pants. Right – yeah – yeah, slide them down! Take 'em off of me!"

As Todd unfastened David's cutoffs, he discovered that David was not wearing any under briefs either, and as the cutoffs slid down just ever so slightly, David's rod sprang out, stiff and into full view. Todd gasped! He kind of moved back, but did not let loose of David, nor his cutoffs that he still had ahold of.

"Oh man! Oh you've got a big hardon man! Oh my! Oh, I wanna touch it! Oh man! – oh man! Oh – I've never done this before! Oh man, I've never touched some other guy's dick! Oh my God it's hard! Oh shit man – it's hard! Oh my God, I'm feeling it man – I'm feeling your dick! Oh, I've never felt some other guy's cock before! Oh, this is weird, this is so weird!"

"Yeah, I know! I know! Reach out. Touch it! Grab your hand on it! Grab around it! Yeah man, yeah! It don't bite! It won't bite you!"

So very, very slowly Todd did reach out for it, and he very slowly took it into his hand. He looked at David and said, "Oh my God man, oh my God, I've got your cock in my hand! I'm holding your cock!"

"Well! How's it feel? Feel OK to you?"

"Oh yeah man, it feels good! It's warm. Oh, I never thought I'd ever get to grab some guy's cock like this! Oh man! Oh man, it feels so funny to have it in my hand like this!"

Todd continued to be rather amused that he was standing there with David's hardon in his hand, as David suggested, "Hey! Bend over and kiss it! Give it a little kiss man!"

Without saying anything, but yet taking about three deep breaths first, Todd did slowly bend over and so very gently and so very slowly he put his tongue out and slightly slid his tongue along the side of the seven inches of stiff meat that David was so anxiously presenting to him.

"Oh yeah – oh yes, that feels so good! Yeah lick it some more! Let me feel your tongue on the side of my dick!"

Without realizing what he was actually doing, Todd suddenly sank down to his knees so that his face was right at the same height as David's dick, and he let the cutoffs fall the rest of the way to the floor. He then grabbed David's hips so that he could pull himself up close, in a much more comfortable position. His face was now positioned directly in front of David's hardon dick!

"Yeah man, yeah!" David encouraged as Todd leaned his face forward and so very cautiously got closer and closer to David's body, and his raging hardon that Todd was now so completely over taken with.

Todd managed to get himself into a rather comfortable position and finally, yes, he finally had the opportunity to play with, feel, stroke and even lick the dick hanging on another man. David simply stood there and let Todd experiment with this new endeavor, for as long as he wanted, and let him do whatever he wanted. David knew this was the moment that Todd had been praying for, for many years, and there was no way now, that he was going to mess it up for him. Once or twice David did need to slightly move his feet so that he was in a more sturdy position, but at no time did he make any comments or make any motions that might indicate to Todd that they needed to do something else. For minutes and more minutes, Todd continued to squat there, directly in front of David's rod and rather worship it as if it was something from another planet or space. So very slowly he licked the side of the cock, and would actually stick his tongue out as far as possible and lick the bushy area around it.

Occasionally David would so very softly place his hand on Todd's head as a signal that everything was feeling good, and to keep doing whatever you want to do. David was encouraging Todd to completely enjoy his new found freedom worshipping the dick on another man!

Todd looked up at David and asked, "Can we go in your bedroom? I want to lay down beside you so I can feel all of you. Can we go do that?"

"Yeah, of course we can!" David quickly replied. "I was just letting you get used to being that close to me and my dick. You looked like maybe you were pretty well enjoying what you were doing there, and I didn't want to stop you."

David stepped out of his cutoffs, which had been laying around his ankles, and with leaving them on the floor, where they landed, he helped Todd stand back up, gave him a firm hug, and an ever so slight of a kiss on the base of his neck and said, "Come on man, let's go back here!"

As they headed down the hallway, David reached over and turned the kitchen light off, and asked Todd, "You still glad you are here? You OK? Everything OK?"

"Oh shit yes I'm glad I'm here and yes everything is OK! I have wanted to do this with some guy for so damn long now that it is hard for me to realize that I am actually headed for bed, with you. I want to lay down with you so I can feel all of you, but I've got to tell you man, you are going to have to take the lead and show me what to do. I know I've wanted to do this for years, but now that it is actually happening, I don't know what to do. I know it's OK, but I'm still kind of scared and I know I don't know what I'm supposed to do!"

David gave him a gentle hug around the waist and said, "Don't worry man, don't worry! I didn't tell you anything to do out there in the kitchen and you sure did everything pretty well out there, so I'm sure you are going to be doing pretty well in here too. Here, let me pull these covers down, and then you lay down there and get comfortable."

Todd did lay down on the bed, and David laid down right beside him as soon as he took his shoes and socks off. Todd was on his back, and David laid down beside him on his stomach, and put his right arm up across Todd's chest.

"Oh shit man! Oh shit!" Todd expressed in a very comforting way. "Oh man, I thought this day would never come! Oh man, please rub my chest, please! Oh man I want to feel your hands go all over me! Oh I've finally got a man doing stuff to my body! Oh man I've dreamt about this happening to me some day! Oh, it's finally happening man, it's finally happening! Oh I've got a man playing with me! Laying here with me, oh man, it's finally happening – it's really happening!"

David did, as he had already planned to do, but Todd's instruction and request just happened to speed the process up a little. David started to slowly move his hand around on Todd's chest, and as the opportunity arose, he would slightly stop, put a finger and a thumb together and so slightly and lovingly pinch one of Todd's tits. Immediately David found out that was a very, very sensuous action for Todd! David knew from many prior experiences that some men like to have their tits played with, and some do not. He had found out that Todd was very definitely a man that loved it.

"Oh man, oh man! Oh that feels so good! Oh man, please do that, again! Oh yeah, pinch it tighter. Yeah please! Yeah, oh I love that!"

Todd was experiencing one of his very first and true sexual pleasures of being with a man, as he so bluntly stated, "Oh man. I've had my tits squeezed before, but man alive, it has never felt like that! Oh shit man, oh man! Oh shit that feels so damn good! Pinch it harder! Yeah harder please! Yeah, let me feel it! Oh, that is so good! Oh man, I love that!"

As Todd was squirming and reacting to the tit action and painful feelings in his sensitive tits of the tighter and tighter pinching, David was finding out very, very quickly that what Todd had mentioned earlier, about maybe thinking that he really needs rough sex, was a true, very possible reality! The only thing, so far, that David had even done to Todd was to pinch his tits, and already Todd was begging for

David to do it rougher, and rougher than what he was already getting. Already, before they had actually had any time to do anything else, he was begging for being treated very roughly and strongly! From his many prior experiences with a number of other bed partners, and some that ended up being floor partners – since they never quite made it to the bed – David already knew that this one, was just at the starting gates of experiencing some completely new and exciting feelings when it comes to his sex play. David could not help but remember the many number of guys, that when he had so very slightly touched their tits, they immediately asked him not to, because it hurt too much! And now, here is Todd, not only asking, but actually begging for it, rougher and rougher, before anything else has even gotten started. David was rather shocked that for a man reacting as strongly and as passionately as Todd was over just having his tits squeezed, that he had not found some way, some man, much earlier to have his body played with and treated the way, that was now becoming a very strong reality, that Todd needed to be treated!

David knew that future times with Todd would involve the need of taking him to Randy' house where there was a much more completely stocked cabinet of some very rough items, yet some very fun items, if a man is willing to be used on the rough and tumble side! He already knew that Todd was one of those men – he just had not had the opportunity to walk that path just yet!

David's idea of letting Todd be the aggressor was now starting to fade into fantasy. Todd's eager pleading for David to get rough with his tits was getting David way too turned on to just lay there and let Todd explore. David flipped himself up and on top of Todd, and with one hand he was pinching Todd's left tit, and on Todd's right tit, he was biting.

"Oh yeah man, Oh yeah! Oh bite that man, yeah, oh yeah! Oh yeah! Oh yeah – Oh yeahhhhhh!" Todd's excitement of being bitten was becoming a complete and definite turn on to David. Suddenly David was realizing that he had not had any man in bed with him for a very long time that was as acceptable to some good, roughing it up action, as this guy was. David was remembering back to the last guy that was even anyplace close to asking for the rough stuff that he had played with, and it was a man that had been roughed up for probably eight or ten years, and even he did not beg for it as much as Todd already was.

Grabbing onto Todd and hugging him up tight around the chest, David moved from tit to tit biting and hearing Todd beg for "More man, yeah, yeah, bite it some more! Oh yeah, bite it tight! Please bite me tight!"

Todd's reaction to this new play was becoming a complete surprise to David. No man, experienced or not, had ever been begging for the pain that he knew Todd had to be feeling as he bit, and he bit tight, on each of Todd's tits.

After almost exhausting himself in the biting actions on Todd's, rather flat tender tits, which David decided certainly would not stay very flat and very tender much longer if Todd continued to have them sucked on and bitten on in such a vigorous way, David started his "face slide" down Todd's chest and gut line.

With both hands firmly grabbing the sides of Todd's upper body, David started sliding down toward Todd's belly button, and as his tongue found its little cavity of space to slide into, David decided to see if some biting action on the edge of Todd's navel was as eagerly accepted as the biting on his tits had been.

As David slightly bit on Todd's navel, he heard the magic sound of Todd expressing another complete acceptance and encouragements of, "Do it more! Oh yeah, do that again!"

With his face now completely buried in Todd's stomach area, his right hand slid down the smooth side of Todd's body and managed to locate the sack of balls that Todd was so proudly hanging under he's raging hardon. David's question of wondering just how much Todd would want those balls played with and just how much force he was willing to accept on them, was quickly answered.

As David grabbed a hold of that bag, Todd almost let out a scream of, "Oh God yes! Oh yeah man, squeeze my nuts! Oh yeah – oh yeah! Oh man – I've wanted some guy to grab my bag and my nuts for years! Oh yeah, yeah – please squeeze 'em! Please, oh yeah, oh let me feel you pull my bag! Squeeze 'em tight!"

Todd's excitement of having David touch him, bite him, grab his bag and pull on it and at the same time squeeze his nuts, was somewhat of a surprise, but was most definitely a complete shock of joy to David. David was getting to experience some new feelings, playing with Todd, as much as Todd was by being played with.

David moved his face down to cock/face position, and while holding the base of Todd's cock with one hand, and squeezing Todd's nuts and pulling on his bag quite firmly, he opened his mouth widely, and took his first great taste of Todd's seven inches, and the almost two inch wide, uncut sausage meat into his mouth, and immediately forced his face down on it, as fully and as completely as he possibly could.

Todd felt David's mouth encompass this dick and immediately let out, with an almost childhood yell of excitement! "Oh my God! Oh my God! – Ohhhh my God!"

Actually throwing his arms in excitement, and thrusting his mid section up into David's face, Todd was beyond the point of excitement! He reached down and grabbed David's head and without even knowing what he was doing, he was forcing his dick and David's head together in a secure and locked embrace.

With his mouth more than fully filled with the "meat of the day," and his face locked up against Todd's body, David was having difficulty in breathing and he had to force his release from Todd's firm grip.

As David managed to break free from the suffocating grip, he looked up at Todd and managed, "Oh man! Oh shit man, I almost suffocated there. Your dick more than fills my mouth and there is no way in hell I could get any air there – and man you had my nose locked up against your gut so tight, I just couldn't get any air through my nose, either! I'm sorry I had to push off of you. I needed some air!"

"Oh shit man I'm sorry! Oh man – your mouth on my dick like that was so damn good – oh man I wanted to put my dick down in you as far as I could go. Oh, I wanted all of me to just slide inside of you! Oh man – I have known for years and years that it must feel great to have some strong guy suck on your dick, but oh man, I never

ever thought it would feel that good. Oh, can you suck on my dick some more and let me feel that again! Oh shit man, I have never felt anything that felt like that before. Oh why in the hell haven't I been getting sucked off by guys for a long time now? Oh shit man, I wish I had done this a long time ago! Oh man, I love this! Oh why didn't I find some guy when I was real young to do this to me? Oh man – oh man, put my dick back in your mouth – please – please! Bite it, bite on it! Yeah please!! Let me feel your teeth on my dick! Yeah, man, yeah – oh yeah, I love that! Oh that feels so good to me! Oh yeah, bite the skin on the end of it! Yeah, yeah oh, I've wanted that done to me for so long! Oh I knew that would feel great! Oh yeah! Oh yeah, bite it harder – yeah, bite me man – bite me!"

David pulled his face back far enough so that he could get his teeth on the foreskin of Todd's dick, and after pulling it out as far a he could tug it, he then bit the skin so very slightly, listening for any signal that his biting was becoming just a little bit too much. The negative comments never came! Just suggestions of a complete acceptance and a begging for "more." Mentally, David was wondering just how much pain this man could and would take. 'Shit man. I know if this was my dick, I'd be telling me to get the hell off of it, and quit biting! How much pain does this guy take?'

After biting the foreskin for quit some time, actually longer than David knew he personally could have taken it, and listening to Todd continue expressing his pleasures of having it bitten, and how good it felt, David pulled his mouth off completely, reached up with both hands and with sliding each thumb in under the loose foreskin, then pinching it with a finger, he pulled and spread the skin out into a bowl shape as far as possible. Then returning his face to the proper face/cock position, he started licking the inside of Todd's foreskin as completely as he could!

"Ohhhh yeah – ohhhhh yeah!" David heard Todd lovingly moan as he started to give his rod that type of intimate care and love that every man deserves.

After his session of treating the inside of Todd's foreskin some very delicate attention, David quickly released his hold on the skin, and once again took Todd's full seven inches down and into the depths of his throat! Once again Todd let out some very loud and very strong expressions of pleasure.

David had now decided that it was finally time for Todd to experience the joy of having a man's mouth work his system to a complete and exciting explosion, the likes of which he has never had before!

The fast and forceful action was now in place, with David's face and mouth working on that dick as strongly and as forcefully as possible, while having his hand completely wrapped around the top of Todd's bag, so that his nuts were forced into the bottom of the bag, and the skin around those balls was pulled up good and tight! David was pulling and grabbing, and Todd was pleading for "More, yeah more!"

David was not just sure which Todd was wanting more of – the cock getting such a sucking, or the bag being pulled as tightly and as strongly as it was. To cover all bases and make sure Todd was getting what he wanted, he sped up the action on Todd's big, major, cock, and at the same time squeezed and pulled his bag even that much stronger!

Suddenly Todd's body started to stiffen up and his ass started raising up off of the bed.

"Oh my God David, I'm about to cum! I'm gonna cummmmm! Oh shit, oh god man – oh I just came man – I just came man – I came!"

As soon as David could manage to swallow everything that had just been dumped into his mouth and down his throat, he attempted to tell Todd, that yes – he knew he came – he was having problems of swallowing all of it fast enough.

"My God man! Holy shit man, do you always dump that much cum when you cum? God man, you are a fucking cow when you dump your cream!"

"I'm sorry! I'm sorry! Really, I didn't even know I was ready to cum yet, and all of a sudden, I lost all control of – everything I guess. Oh man! I know my arms were flying weren't they? I know I was doing some stupid stuff that I never do. Shit man, that climax was so damn hot that I know I must have been jumping and hollering and stuff. Wasn't I? Oh man, you pulling on my bag like that was unbelievable man! What a great feeling! Hell, if I had ever known about that and how it felt, I'd been tying my bag to a bedpost or something and pulling on it when I jerked off! Man, I've never felt that before! Wow – what a climax! God I love to have my bag and nuts pulled on like that! Man, what a feeling!"

Todd's excitement of being treated, in David's mind, like a "Real Man" was very exciting to him. He truly appreciated the fact that he was in bed with a man that liked it on the rougher side, even though, and especially since, it was Todd's first time with a man.

Re-composing himself from all of the mouth actions and the heavy breathing that he had just accomplished, David sat up straddling Todd's legs and told him, "Well, man, I know for sure that you are probably totally wiped out and exhausted after all of the energy that you just shot out of the end of your dick, so just lay there and relax. I'm going to scoot up on you, and after I get up there with my crotch right under your chin, I'm going to let you see what my dick tastes like, and let you see what a great feeling it is to have a mouth full of meat, some meat that did not come from your local supermarket! You ready for this man?"

"Oh yeah man, I am! Oh yeah I want to suck and chew on your dick! Yeah, yeah please scoot up here and let me have your dick. Oh my God, oh my day is finally here! Oh man I can't believe it! I finally get to take a guy's cock in my mouth! Oh, fuck my mouth, please! Push your dick down in my mouth David! Yeah, yeah – do it – do it!"

CHAPTER FOUR:

Tie Me Up Man, Tie Me Up

David was sitting with his crotch right at Todd's chin, and with one great big assed grin on his face, David raised up, pushed his rod down, aimed it for Todd's anxious mouth and pushed it in. His position was not the best for combining a dick that wants to head north, and a throat that is definitely headed south.

After just a moment or two, David pulled his dick back out and told Todd, "Hey man. This position is not working so well. My dick is not going down in your throat this way. Scoot down in the bed. Let me turn around here and we'll do the good ole 69 thing."

Todd scooted down, David turned around and got himself into position so that his dick and Todd's mouth had a precisely placed happy union, just perfectly placed so that David could just move his dick ever so slightly and let Todd take it in as quickly or as slowly as he wanted.

Quickly was the mode of action when David laid his head down on Todd's already once, exhausted dick of death. It was not completely soft, but yet it was not as rigid as it had been only moments before when Todd let fly with all of the cum that David thought perhaps maybe three guys should have been involved in, due to it's abundant supply that he attempted to swallow!

Todd's actions on taking as much of David's dick as possible was much more quickly accomplished than David had expected. Knowing that Todd had never had a man's dick in his mouth before, let alone even handling one in his hand, he did not expect Todd to immediately go for the whole thing, right at once. Wrong! Wrong! Once again, Todd was surprising the hell out of David in what he was willing to do, and the way he was willing to do it! Taking David's cock was being done the same way Todd had begged for getting his tits pinched, tighter and tighter. No hesitation! He was in a position now of having a man's stiff rod pushed into his mouth, and he had decided that there was no way he was going to imply that maybe he either did not want to do this, or that maybe he shouldn't be doing it at all. Todd was finally in his glory, and he was going to take advantage of it, and not miss one opportunity of doing everything that he has dreamed about doing for the past number of years. He was finally getting cock, and he was finally giving cock, and there was no way he wanted this to stop! He knew this action was really letting him know that he really was a gay guy, since this sex was so much more exciting and a hell of a lot hotter than with Julie, but now, he was feeling like tonight, for the first time, that he had just become a true man! He knew that his natural being, required rough and tumble sex for him to really enjoy it, and this was what he was getting with David. With Julie, is was just the lay there, fuck, climax, roll over and go to sleep. With David, it was contact, feeling, roughing, slamming, pocking, pinching, tugging, squeezing, biting, and every other feeling and emotion that he knew he had not even yet experienced.

It had not been mentioned yet, nor talked about even, but as he laid there taking David's meat down into his throat and realizing that he was finally doing what he had always been destined to do, he fantasized about the men he had read about that were tied down, totally restrained and controlled, as they had their mouth fucked or their ass fucked. The whole idea of being restrained and not being able to move, giving himself to some other guy to use, to his complete desires, either in his mouth, up his ass or in whichever and whatever fashion that playmate wanted, was definitely a hot, exciting, turn on to Todd. He had been wanting to feel that unexplainable feeling of total submissiveness for a long time, and tonight he was getting really close to the whole idea of just giving his entire body to David, without having any say about what was going to happen.

With this tie down, and total submissive idea in his mind, his entire body got active. His head started jerking up and down trying to get more and more of David into his mouth, and at the same time his midsection went into overdrive, giving David's mouth, a rod that really needed to be sucked on, chewed on, and bitten on, again. David knew something was happening that was making Todd so animated. He knew Todd was getting excited about something more than just what was happening in the bed right then.

David pulled off of Todd's dick, looked back at Todd, and asked, "What's up man? What's happening?"

Without actually even thinking about what he was saying, Todd blurted out, "Tie me up man, I want to be tied up and have you fuck me!"

David was shocked, but gained a very big grin on his face as he uttered a quick, "OK." Shocked, he was, but willing – he was that and also thinking, 'God, this guy is no fucking virgin at this shit!' He thought to himself. 'If he is, he sure as hell has been hiding his true self, from himself for way too long! This guy is a fucking tiger in bed with another guy! Love it! Love it, but just fucking totally unexpected!'

David then got up, looked back at Todd and said, "Can do man, definitely can do! You are sure, though? You want me to tie you down and play with you, right? Todd, I don't want to do stuff that is going to make you decide you've gone too far! You sure you want me to tie you up and fuck you?"

"Oh God yeah! Oh yeah, I do! Man I've got to admit that I'm even surprised that I even said that, but yeah – I said it and I meant it. While I was sucking on your dick – which I swear to God was the hottest damn thing I have ever done in my entire life, I got to thinking about some stories that I've read about the guys that get tied down, and how they couldn't do anything except just lay there and take whatever the other guy decided to do to them, and all of a sudden I wanted to be tied down by you and have you use me! Probably face fuck me! Oh, is that sick or anything? I mean, is that a normal thing for a guy to want? Man, I've got to tell you, I hope like hell it is OK, cause if not, I'm one fucking bastard because I want it! And I want it bad! I want you to fuck around with me anyway you want! Oh, my God, I never thought I'd get this damn hot when playing with a guy! Man, this is way more than I ever expected it to be! Shit man, why in the hell didn't I find someone to fuck around with me like this a long time ago! Oh, yeah – I'm yours. Tie me up! Use me, do stuff to me! This is way too fucking fun, man! I love this! Will you tie me up and do stuff to me? Play with me and make me feel like those guys did that I read about? Oh yeah, I've wanted to just give myself to some guy for so long now, yeah, I want this! Yeah, I want to know that – well – I don't know – I know this is weird, but I guess I want to know that I just let myself be all played with by some guy! You will, won't you please?"

"Shit yes! Hell yes I will man! Damn, you don't have to ask me twice! When I have you tied down on the bed, I'm going to fuck your ass, I know I am! With you tied down, that is going to make a ragging maniac out of me wanting to do stuff to you, so you do know – you are going to get my dick rammed up in your ass, right?"

"Oh yeah I know! I know right now, I know I am probably the dumbest guy in the world for just saying yeah, I know, and telling you to do it, but, I want to be like the guys that I have read about and know that I can get fucked in the ass like those guys can! Just don't tear me up too bad when you fuck it, OK? I know it's going to hurt like hell, I already know that! But I am so fucking horny for doing stuff that I've never done before that I'm willing to let you do whatever, just so I can say I did that! I know other guys can get big dicks stuck up in their asses, and I want to know that I can do that too! Fuck me, yeah tie me up so I can't get up and out from under you, and then fuck me! Oh God! Those dildos you've got! Oh man – oh shit man! Oh, will you fuck my ass with one of those long ones please? Oh God man, I almost forgot about those things. I really want you to fuck my ass with that long one, please?! Oh man, how could I forget you've got those? Shit man, they're the whole reason I'm even here!"

"OK man, I'm willing if you are! Turn over on your gut man, and spread your arms and legs out!"

As Todd flipped over and got himself in position to be tied down, face down, David retrieved four leather straps that were in his bedside drawer, and starting with the wrists, he tied each wrist and then each ankle to the bed frame.

David reached over to the bed stand, removed a leather blindfold, and told Todd, "We're gonna do you like a true slave boy is treated – I'm gonna blindfold you so that you can only imagine just what is going on back here. Tied down, helpless and now blindfolded, you are gonna get to have the best first time gay fucking in your ass that any man, I mean any man, has ever had! Todd, you're shaking man, but trust me, OK? You're OK! I won't do anything to you that I shouldn't – but tonight is the only time that you're ever gonna be able to call this your first time, and I want you to know you are getting it all the way! You are definitely into some hot gay sex man – some hot gay sex!" He then checked with Todd that everything was OK and nothing had been tied too tight, to where, either his wrist nor, his ankles were hurting.

"Oh no man! No, I'm fine. Got to admit feeling pretty weird here though. I've never been tied down by somebody to where I was completely helpless, and of course totally naked and bare assed, let alone knowing that I'm about to get my ass fucked and played with this way. God man, I hope like hell I am not out of my mind for telling you I wanted this. Do all gay guys act like I am? Do all you guys like to be tied down and played with like this, or am I just fucking crazy?"

"No definitely, no! In fact a big no! No, you are not crazy, but no, I've got to admit that most guys don't ask to get tied down the first time they have gay sex. I've got to admit that having you begging for this – the very first time you've played, and especially for your very first ass fucking – this is really way off of the wall of normal. I've never had any guy even imply he had ideas of getting tied up to get fucked before, let alone some virgin assed guy! Todd, you are really one of a kind, I guess. You still game for this, or since you're all tied up and can't move, are you wanting to change your mind?"

"I'm wonder just how fucking crazy I am man, but I said I wanted this, and I'm not going to back out now. All I ask is that you remember I'm just a normal guy, and I've never had anybody do anything to my ass before, so just please don't tear me up? Please make sure I can take it before you force your dick up in me, OK?"

"Hey, I already know you can take it! When a guy can get a fist rammed up in his ass, I know a guy can get a dick rammed up in his ass."

"Yeah – I know, I know, but I've never had a fist rammed up in me either!"

"Yeah, I know! I didn't mean this ass, I didn't mean your ass, I just meant in general. What I was trying to say is – your ass might feel pretty closed and tight right now, but just give us a little time, and we will get it open. OK? Lay there and try to relax, man. I'm going to start doing some playing back here, and just pretty soon, we are going to have your ass so full of my dick and then one of those big dildos, you will not believe what your ass can really take or do. You just lay there and try and relax that ass!"

As David told Todd to just lay there and relax that ass, he positioned his face right above Todd's two very lovable butt bubbles, and with ever so slightly spreading them apart, he placed his face right down in the middle of them, and started giving Todd some tongue licking and some ass sucking, as of course, Todd had never experienced before. He had his lips pushed up tight to Todd's ass skin and after pulling his ass checks apart some, blew some air up and into Todd's ass. He licked the edge of Todd's ass and slid his tongue across Todd's left ass cheek as he pulled back.

"Oh man, – oh shit man, that feels so fucking good! Oh man, are you actually licking on my asshole? Oh I've never felt anything like that before! Oh – oh my God man! Oh shit man – that is so fucking hot! You blew air up and in my ass didn't you? You actually blew some air into my ass! Oh man I never thought about some guy doing that to me! Oh wow! Oh shit! Oh man, that is so hot! Oh man,

I can't believe you actually had your tongue up in my ass! Oh shit man, this is great!"

After giving Todd the feeling of his life by licking and kissing not only on his butt, but down, and as deep in it, as far as he could push his face, David then told Todd to just lay there and relax, that he was going to smear some lube on his ass, and then stick a finger or two up in there.

"So you just lay there and remember, I've done this to other guys before, and they're all up and walking around, so your ass is safe. Yeah, I admit, you are going to have some feelings back here like you've never felt before, but by the time we are all done, you are going to be one happy guy that you let me play with your ole butt hole."

"Oh man, I hope so, I hope so. With you playing around back there and feeling your fingers going in, I'm really wondering just how fucking crazy I am tonight! But oh man, if it feels anything close to what it felt like when you were licking back there, I'm all game man, I'm all game. Scared shitless, I admit, but I'm the one that asked for it, so man, now I've got to be man enough to do it! Oh shit man, I know that when I told you I needed to come back over here to schedule the carpet thing, I knew then why I wanted to come back so badly, but oh man, now I'm really wondering just how fucking crazy I am. Please don't hurt me! Please! Please go slow, David!"

"Hey, you lay there and you let me take care of this end, and everything will be OK. Understand me man? You sure as the hell are not the first guy to get his ass fucked and played with, and tonight, sure as the hell is not going to be your last time of doing it, either! Yeah, it's different and something that you've never let somebody do to you before, but by the time it's all over, you are going to be making sure you can get it again!"

As Todd managed to lay calmly – well as calmly as any guy can that knows he is about to have stuff stuck up in his ass, and an ass that has never been played with like this before, David started a little finger action. He started with just one finger. He wanted Todd to feel the movement of just the one finger and see what something flexible could feel like stuck up in there. As he had the first finger inserted, he then massaged the inside of Todd's ass.

"Oh man! Oh shit, man, that feels so damn good! Yeah man, finger me! Yeah, do that man, yeah!"

Todd was definitely feeling the good side of having a guy's finger up in his ass feeling around and rather playing the good game in there.

David pulled the one finger out, and replaced it with two. An even more excited reaction came from Todd! "Oh my God David, Oh my God that is great! Oh shit man, oh shit!"

After having the two fingers inserted, David then removed those two, and replaced them with the tips of four fingers, two from his left hand, and two from his right hand.

"Oh shit man! Oh man, what you doing down there? Oh man that feels funny. David, what're you doing?"

"I'm just kind of spreading stuff open a little back here, that's all. You just lay there and let me get this back door all open and ready for my ragging hardon rod, because I am just about ready to take your asshole virginity away from you. I'm just kind of pulling your asshole open a little, so you just lay there and let me do my thing, OK?"

"Yeah – OK! Yeah, it just feels so funny though! Yeah, OK, yeah. You going to tell me when you are going to fuck me? You going to tell me when you are going to ram my ass with your dick?"

"Yeah – sure I will and it is right now!"

Suddenly David let loose of Todd's ass, adjusted his position and as he was telling Todd that he was about to get it in the ass, he put his cock meat right at Todd's back door and started in.

"Lay still, I'm starting to fuck you man! You are finally going to get a dick up in your ass. Lay still!"

"Oh my God, oh my God I can feel that! Oh David go slow, slow, slow!"

"I am man – I am! Oh – there! There, I just went in! You OK? I just put my dick in your ass! Hey man, you can no longer say you've never been fucked in the ass! You have now got another man's dick up in your butt hole! My cock is in your ass! Another man is up inside of you now man – yes I am! Yeah man – I'm in you!"

"Oh God man, yeah – I'm OK but just lay there a minute please. Oh, it did hurt for just a second when I felt you push in me! Oh man, I've really got your dick up in me now, don't I? I have been fucked now, haven't I?"

"Yeah man, yes you do, and yes you have been! Your time of saying I've never been fucked in the ass before is now, time gone by. You've got a guy in your butt. You just lay there. Since I'm in now, now it's just see how far up in you I can go. You just lay there and enjoy this, because that is exactly what you are going to do. Once the dick slips in past that first muscle, then it is feeling good time all the rest of the way!"

Todd quickly did realize that getting fucked in the butt was probably even more exciting and thrilling than he had even imagined it would be, whenever he managed to finally get it done. Now that the time was finally here, the idea of being completely restrained with the leather straps, submitting himself so completely to another man and having no self control over anything that was happening, feeling David's body laying fully nude the entire length of his own nude body, and of course the ever important part of knowing that another man has his dick up in his ass, and the great, great feelings that dick was delivering, was creating a much greater sense of enjoyment, than Todd had ever thought could be.

Laying there, having his body pounded on by a man that had gotten more and more excited as he started fucking this virgin ass, Todd was finally getting what he had prayed for for years! He was being fucked! He was finally getting fucked!

"Oh my God man, fuck me – fuck me hard! Ram it, ram it, ram it!!! Oh, I'm finally getting fucked! Oh man fuck me hard! Let me feel your big dick up in me man – yeah fuck the hell out of me! Oh man, make me remember this always! Make me feel it more than any other guy has ever felt getting his ass fucked! Oh, David make me part of you!"

Todd's excitement was more than David could handle.

"Oh man, I'm gonna cumm man, I'm gonna cum! Oh, I'm about to cuuumm! Yeah man, oh man, here it cummms! I'm cumin man, I'm cummmmin'! Oh fuck man, oh fuck! Oh shit man you are getting a whole bunch of juices shot up in your ass! Todd man, you have just gotten hard cock cum shot up in you! Oh yeah! Can you feel it? Can you feel my cum juices up inside of you?"

"Oh yeah, yeah I can! It's warm, it feels real warm up in there!"

As David completely, and thoroughly shot every bit of his warm man juices that he had – which he had been building up for a few days in hopeful anticipation that this night might turn out something like this, he was totally exhausted and fell lifeless down on Todd's back.

With Todd being tied down four pointed, both arms spread out and tied to the bed frame and both legs also being tied tight, David laid across Todd as if he was tied down on top of him.

"Hey man, how you feeling?" David quietly asked as he enjoyed the feeling of Todd under him and yet the feeling of his dick still stuck up in Todd's tight, hot, ass.

"Oh man I can't explain it! This is feeling something that I never expected! Oh, I love this! I did not know it could be this good! Of all of the stories that I have read about a guy getting fucked, none of them ever really made me really understand just what it really felt like! Oh please don't ever pull out of me or get off of me. I want to lay here like this forever! Oh why in the hell was I ever scared of getting a dick rammed up in my ass? Shit man, there ain't nothing better than this! Oh crap I wish I had been doing this for years and years now! I tell you, I'm not going to want to have sex with Julie anymore. She's not going to be able to do for me what you just did for me. No way man, no way!"

CHAPTER FIVE:

"Yeah Todd, Yeah You Do!"

Still laying on top of Todd, David lowered his head down beside Todd's ear and softly whispered, "Which dildo do you want first?"

"Oh my God, oh shit man – you gonna use one of those on me?"

"Well, yeah man, yeah. I thought you wanted one of them up in you! Isn't that why you came over here tonight?"

"Oh yeah, yeah! Yeah it is man, well anyway, it sure was a good way to let you know I wanted to do something, but man after that fucking I just got, you think I can take a dildo up in there now? You think I can do that?"

"Hell yeah man, hell yeah! Your ass just got fucked, not cemented shut! Hell man, you let me run that 15 incher up in there and you may never want me to take it back out!"

"Oh shit, how many dildos you got? I saw two the other day. Is that all you got or you got more?"

"Tell you what young man. You lay there and hug that bed and let me use that asshole of yours and I'll just start with the smallest one and move up the line. OK? Hell – tell you what. Think I'll fuck your cute tight little butt with a dildo, then use my dick in there, then put in another dildo, then fuck you again and just kind of do that for awhile, until you tell me you and your cute little hole have had enough for one night! OK? OK if I do that?"

"Oh shit man, yeah! Oh David, that sounds so hot to me! Yeah do that! Yeah, do that!"

With Todd's emphatic insistence that David do use the dildos, then use his own dick and then another dildo, David reached over to the bed stand and took out the smallest and skinniest of the dildos he had available. It was 15 inches long and only about four and a half inches around.

After smearing some Crisco on the dildo, David aimed it toward Todd's ass and said, "OK man, dildo number one! Just lay there and relax. Seriously man, this one is so skinny, you probably won't even hardly feel it going up in you!"

Todd laid there, still fully tied down with both arms stretched out and tied, and both legs stretched out and tied and blindfolded! Anxiously he asked, "Oh man, how long is it? How big is it!?"

"Hey Todd, like I said men, it's skinny but it's long enough that we'll be able to let you take a little bit of length, just to prove to you that you've got a deep asshole back here. Lay still there and just let me slide this up and in, OK?"

Calmly Todd said, "OK," and so slightly, and even without realizing what he was doing, he attempted to push his butt up in the air as if to say, "I'm hungry, my butt's hungry, and I want that! Put that up in me!"

David started the slide into Todd's ass. Todd simply laid there and made no comments other than a couple of pleasant "Ahs" and a few "Yes." David could tell and did know that Todd was easily taking this tool up in his ass, and was taking it very quickly!

"Yeah man! Yeah man! Yeah, I can feel that going up in me. Yeah that feels good! Hey man, how much is up in me? How much you put in me?"

"Well, this one is 15 inches long, and right now I've only got enough left out of you so that I can keep a hand on it, so I'd say that right now you have 12 or 13inches of dildo up in you! How's that sounding to that tight little ass of yours?"

"Oh my God, you serious? I can't have 12 or 13 inches of that up in me, do I? Shit man! I can't have that much up in there, do I?"

"Yeah – yes you do! Surprise you? Didn't think you could do that did you?"

"Shit no, hell no! You sure! Really – I have something that long up in my ass? I really have 12 or 13 inches of that up in me right now? Really? Oh my God man! I can't believe I've got something that long up inside of me!"

"You sure do man! You sure do! Tell you what. I'm gonna put my finger right here, on the dildo, where your asshole is at, and keep it on the dildo until after I pull it all out of you, pull your blindfold off, and then show you how much you had up inside, OK?"

David did. With his finger firmly planted on the side of the dildo, he then slowly started pulling it back out of Todd's ass. As it came out, and Todd's little butt hole slid back shut, David leaned forward with the dildo in hand and said, "Hey, look! Here, this is what was up in you, and this is where your asshole was when I started pulling it back out! Pretty impressive, right? You've got one hungrier asshole than you thought, don't you?"

"Oh man, really, really? I really had that much up inside of me? I really couldn't hardly feel it! Shit man, I thought sticking something that long up in your ass would hurt like hell! I felt it, kind of up in there, but not like it was that far up in me! Really man, really I had that much up in me?"

"Sure did, and now it's time for my little massaging of the ole asshole. Remember, I said I was gonna use a dildo on you, then fuck you for a minute or two, then use another dildo?"

"Yeah yeah! I remember! Yeah fuck me man, fuck me and fuck me hard! Yeah, your dick in me feels so fucking good man, so fucking good! Oh yeah man, oh yeah, fuck me!"

David took advantage of his position in Todd's butt hole and did as Todd was begging. He fucked him good and hard, and good and rough!

"Oh God, yeah! Oh man that feels so good!"

"Hang tight Todd, I'm gonna cum again man! Man, oh man, I can't believe this! Oh shit man, I thought I just unloaded in you a few minutes ago. Oh my God Todd – I'm cummmmmin' man – I'm cummmmmin'!"

Much to his surprise, but with great pleasure, David dumped his man cream juices up in Todd's ass – again! "Oh God, man I can not believe I came again so fast! Shit man, I guess playing with you like this has got me really hot and horny! Man, it's been years since I've cum twice, that fast, that close together! Shit man! Let's get another dildo stuck up in your ass and see if I get still more excited this time too."

After regaining his breath some, David again reached over to the bed stand and took out another dildo. This one measured 18 inches long and was a little thicker, measuring five and a half inches around. David greased it up well and also smeared some additional Crisco on, and up into, Todd's ass.

"Here man! Here's your next one!" David reached down and after sliding a couple of fingers into Todd's ass and moving them around for a minute or two, he pulled his fingers out and started the tip of the dildo up and into Todd's ass.

"Oh yeah! Oh yeah! Yeah, I can feel that one. Hey, oh, oh, go slow! Yeah, I can feel that one! That one's a lot bigger then the other one, right?"

"No not really. Not too much! Just lay there and relax your butt and let me move this up and in you real slowly. Now if it does get uncomfortable, let me know, but I think you'll take it all OK. Yeah, here, let me do you."

"Oh yeah man, I can feel it! Go slow, but yeah, keep pushing, keep pushing! Yeah, I can feel it. Yeah man, I can feel it moving up in me! It feels good! Yeah push, push! Oh yeah, I feel that going up in me. Oh, that feels good! Yeah, man, I like this, yeah I like this!"

Without any need of asking Todd how he was doing, David continued his slow and careful imbedding of the dildo up and into Todd's ass.

"Oh, how much have I got up in me? How much I got up in me?"

"Well, let me tell you man, you are taking it pretty fast. How much you think you got up in there?"

"Oh, I don't know. What, three inches, maybe four? That much?"

"Oh hell yeah man, hell yeah! You think you've only got four inches up in you? Serious?"

"Yeah! Why? Have I got more than that up in there?"

"Yeah – man, yeah! You sure as hell do! You have four inches up in there, but the only thing is, there's another seven or eight more with it! Really! Right now you've got just about 12 inches of this thing up in your butt! Can't you feel it up in there?"

"Yeah, I can feel it, but I didn't think it was that much! Oh yeah, this feels good to me, really! I'm really kind of wondering if I'm normal or not. Seriously man, I love this! I thought something that long up in my ass should hurt like hell. It feels good! Oh, just knowing I'm all tied down to the bed, I've got you back there playing with my ass, and I've got that much dildo stuck up in my ass is just making me crazy man, just fucking crazy! I love this! Yeah man, yeah! Play with me – play with me – play with me! Oh yeah man! Play with my ass!"

Being very careful, yet very playful, David played with the dildo, by pushing and pulling it in and out, ever so slightly, so that Todd could experience the great feelings of being very deeply fucked – true – by a dildo, but none the less – getting to experience that very deep feeling of intrusion, way up inside of his body.

After about ten minutes of David letting Todd enjoy the new feelings of now having something stuck up in his ass, and actually managing to put in an additional two inches more of the dildo, he told Todd that he was going to start pulling it back out, and once again he'd show him just how much thick, dildo dick, he had taken.

After slowly and rather playfully removing the dildo from Todd's ass, David once again said, "Hey. Look! This is what you had up inside of you!"

Holding out the dildo so that Todd could turn his head and see it, David held his finger tip at the spot where Todd's asshole had been, just before David removed it.

"Oh shit man! Are you serious David? I had all that up in me? Oh crap man! All that?"

You sure did man, you sure did! Your ass is one fucking hungry hole! I can just about tell you right now that the way that ass of yours is acting, you are one man headed toward getting fisted one day, soon. Seriously, you are taking these so easily, and especially for being your first time getting anything up in your ass, I can tell that pretty soon, you are gonna be looking for more and bigger stuff to take up in there. Every guy that is now a fister or a fistee, had to start out somewhere, and I think you are making a pretty good start today!"

"Hey, that one you just took out of me. It's got two heads on it, right? One on each end?"

"Yeah, it does. It's a double headed dildo! Designed for two guys, or well two people – guess a gal could be involved, anyway, to use it at the same time and each person takes part of it and then they let their butts come together while they are both getting fucked in the butt! Never done that with some gal, but sure have done it with a number of guys, and it's fun! Course, with you, right now, I'd be afraid you'd take all of it and leave me with about one inch or so!"

"Oh yeah – right! I don't think so, but if you say so, man! Just the idea of doing that sounds fucking hot to me! Can we do that sometime? Never thought about doing that, but I like the sounds of that! Yeah man, that sounds hot!"

"Sure man, sure we can sometime. I like the way you play! I'm kind of looking forward to a lot of future play with you if you want!"

"Oh shit yeah man! Hell yeah! You are teaching me and showing me stuff tonight that I never thought I'd ever get to do. Yeah man! Yeah, I want to do a lot of future playing! I love this!"

"Well, how's you ass feeling now? You wanting more? Or, are you feeling done, after taking that one up in there?

"No I'm not done! No! I mean – if we can do some more, I want to! But hey, it's not up to me. But – if – you want to, I'm still game! I'm living man – I'm living!"

"Hey if your ass is up to it, so am I! Hang on man, I'm gonna poke you again and let my little ole dick have some fun in that hot ass of yours, then we'll go for the next dildo. OK?"

"Yeah, yeah, OK! Yeah, fuck me! Oh, I can't believe this! Oh man I am so fucking glad I got up enough nerve to come over here tonight. Really man, I've read about guys doing stuff like this, and I've wanted to do something like this for years. Thanks for helping me do this stuff. Thanks man, thanks a lot!"

David aimed his dick, and immediately took his desired position down deep into Todd's ass.

"Oh shit man! Oh God that feels so fucking good! Oh man! You'd think after having that other dildo stuck up in my ass that my ass would be standing wide open, but oh man, your dick feels so good up in there! Fuck me man, fuck me!"

David did! He took advantage of one eager, anxious and hungry ass. He humped and pumped Todd's butt as if there had never been anything up in there yet that night. After about six or seven minutes of ass pounding, David suddenly laid down on Todd's back and said, "OK man, it's time for something bigger than me up in there. Todd, I kind of think maybe we need to untie you and have you turn over onto your back before you take this next one. We need to get you into a position so that you can kind of squirm and move around a little if you need to. This one's gonna take a little more concentration and maybe some teeth gritting to get it up in you where we want it."

Cautiously Todd said. "OK. OK." He was not just so sure of why David had suggested that, but he was definitely doing anything that David suggested, or said they needed to do.

After getting untied and turned over onto his back, Todd watched David as he reached over to the night stand, and removed another dildo.

"Oh shit man! Oh God! You're not gonna use that one on me – are you? Oh shit man that one's fucking big! Oh my God, I don't know if I can take that one or not! God man it's big! Oh shit man, how much bigger is that than the one I just had in me? Oh fuck man, that one looks so fucking big!"

"Well, the last one was about five and a half inches around and about 18 inches long, and this one is seven inches around but only about 15 inches down to the balls. If we can get all of this up in you so your ass is up against those balls, you will really like that! With this much dick up inside and then having someone pushing up against your ass with these big balls on this thing, it feels great. But first, we need to see if we can get this up in you. Ready? Still willing? This is one of those dildos you saw the other day when I left them laying out! Hey man, it's because of this baby that you're even here, so you better take it and love it! OK?"

"Oh God man, it looks so fucking big now! Really, do you really think I can get that up in my ass?"

"Got to be honest man, I really don't know, but in a minute or two, we'll find out. I'm gonna play with your ass a little and just finger it open a little more so we can get this one started up in there. Lay still and just relax. I'm gonna grease you and this dildo up real good."

Just as soon as David got some grease on the dildo and on Todd's ass, he fingered Todd's ass and attempted to open it up a little wider, by slightly pulling it open with his fingers, and he then started the bigger dildo in.

"Oh shit, oh my God! Oh, it feels so fucking big! David you sure it's not a whole lot bigger than only seven inches around? The other one was five and a half, right? Man, only an inch and a half bigger shouldn't be that much bigger, is it? Oh, I don't know! It feels so fucking big!"

"Relax man, relax! This one is bigger and it's gonna stretch your little asshole a little more. Let's take it slow and see how much of it we can get up in there."

For more than five or six minutes, Todd forced himself to just lay there, he kept taking big deep breaths, and tried to keep his ass relaxed and take as much dildo as he could, each time David pushed on it.

"Doing good man! You're doing good! It's going slow, but we're making head way. Feeling pretty full in there, isn't it?"

"Oh God yes! Yes it does! Oh, I can't believe how much bigger this one feels, as opposed to that other one! This one is really stretching me, I can tell! How much you got in me? Tell me, how am I doing?"

"You're doing good! You are doing real good! I'm serious, you are taking this thing a hell of a lot faster than I've ever seen any guy take it for his first time, and especially since tonight is the very first time you've ever had anything stuck up in that ass. You are one anxious asshole. I'm serious! You are gonna be getting yourself fisted sooner than you think. The way your ass is anxious for whatever I can give it, that's showing just what you have in store for you in the future!"

"Hey, how much is up in me? How's it going?"

"You've got just about three fourth of it up in there. You're taking it like a pro! You feeling up to trying to take the last three or four inches, so you can see what having those balls pushed up against your ass feels like? You doing OK?"

"Oh yeah, I'm doing OK! Never, never thought I'd ever be taking something like this up in my ass, especially tonight! Oh man! When I came over here, I never expected anything like this to happen. Really, I don't know what I thought would happen, but man, I sure as hell never thought I'd be doing this. Yeah, I want to see it I can get the rest of it up in me. You think maybe I can?"

"Hey man – right now – knowing how fucking anxious your ass is and has been tonight, I'm about ready to get my Ram Truck and drive it up in there! Yeah, lay there and let me keep working on it! You'll take it! You're doing good! Once we got in past that one spot that gave you some problems, it's been free sailing all the way since then. Yeah it's been going in a little slower than the other ones, but I've been watching your face, and I could tell every time how happy you were when it slid in just a little bit farther. Every time it moved up in you, you broke out in a big smile! Yeah, I know you feel like it's been a challenge, but seriously man, you have taken this thing fast! Lay still, take a big deep breath, let me push it the rest of the way!"

"Oh, I've got it all don't I? Are those the balls I feel pushing on my ass? Did I take all of it? Oh yeah, push on it! Oh yeah man, let me feel those balls pushing on my ass! Oh man that feels so good! Yeah – I did it! Yeah – I did it! I did it – didn't I?"

"Yeah, yes you did! You need to be pretty fucking proud of yourself! Pretty fucking proud! You do better than most guys I've played with that have been getting fucked for years! You do good!"

After some good pushing and playing around so that Todd could really take a good advantage of having the big balls now slamming up against his ass, and having the shaft of that dildo pushing up against everything inside of him, David asked if he was ready to let his ass rest for the rest of the night. Todd said that he really didn't want to, but he also knew that whatever time it was, regardless of how late it was, or even how long they had already played, he knew he wouldn't be ready to stop.

"Oh, go slow, yeah slow! Yeah pull it out slow! Oh man! I can feel it coming back out more than I felt it going in. Yeah slow, slow, slow! Oh, what a fucking feeling! Wow, shit man! I felt my ass slam shut when that came out! Oh what a fucking feeling! I think maybe we have done about enough for one night, but man, please tell me we can do this again, and again real soon! Oh, I can not believe what we just did! Thanks man, thanks! I guess I might as well admit it right now, I'm into doing guys, and letting guys do me. Sex has never been this great before! Thanks! Man – you have shown me the real me tonight! Now I know what great sex is like, and I like it! Oh, I just hope I can show some guys how to have some great sex just like you showed me tonight! Man, oh man! Boy am I gonna have some fucking trouble being in here around you trying to lay carpet in a couple of days with my co-workers here and me trying to act normal. Oh God man! Please don't have anything sexy on! Please keep your shirt on and please don't wear any sexy looking shorts! Oh, don't make me want to jump your bones that day! Oh fuck! I know I'm gonna have some real trouble trying to keep my mind on laying carpet that day!"

CHAPTER SIX:

"This Off Base for You?"

Waiting for somebody to answer his knock at the front door, Todd rather anxiously stepped, back and forth, from foot to foot, wondering if anybody was at home. Mrs. Wilson had asked him to come, at this particular time, to finish up the installation details.

Finally Todd heard somebody, from inside, yell that he'd be right there. Hearing the front door being unlocked, it opened up and Todd was greeted by a young man. He had been expecting Mrs. Wilson to be the person to answer the door.

"Oh hi, I'm Gary. You're the carpet guy I guess, right?"

"Yes, I am. Mrs. Wilson asked that I stop back at this time to finish up the small amount of detailing that needs to be finished. Is she here by chance?"

"No she's not. She and Dad found out at the last minute that they needed to meet with their lawyer, so she asked me to be here so you could come in and do whatever you need to do. Yeah – like I said, I'm Gary, their son. Come on in. Sorry took me so long to get to the door. I was down in the basement lifting some weights and I like to workout in the nude whenever I'm home alone, so had to grab some shorts before I could get the door. Sorry!"

"Hey, no need to be sorry! I'm Todd Underwood. Your Mom asked me if I could stop by today and finish this up, so since it's Saturday, I don't really look like I'm from the carpet place. Their stupid uniforms, I can only stand them for five days a week, and since I thought I'd be recognized as the same guy, I don't look very official."

"Hey man, not a problem with me! You look quite OK, and besides I knew somebody was supposed to be here from the carpet store anyway, so really, some stupid uniform ain't necessary anyway! Come on in."

Todd stepped in as Gary stepped back and held the door open so that Todd could manager the piece of carpeting and his tools. As he stepped into the front area of the house, Todd did ever so slightly did attempt to just – kind of – ever so accidentally – ever so slightly, just happen, to brush his right hand up against the bulge that Gary was showing so proudly. Todd was hoping, anyway, that he was showing so proudly, and on purpose! His attempt to ever so slightly, let the back of his hand slide smoothly and innocently over the bulge, did not quite happen. Todd was disappointed. As he had fumbled and stumbled in his attempt to tell Gary why he was there at that time and why he was not in uniform clothes, he had done a very quick and complete inventory of the young weightlifter that was standing there in front of him, with virtually nothing on! A pair of tennis shoes – no socks, a pair of very exciting, very short, and very tight, shorts – no jock strap – obviously – and of course, no shirt.

Having now gotten himself inside, and had set some of his cargo down on the floor, Todd turned to Gary, and just as Gary closed the door, he extended his hand, and said. "Hey, did not feel like we met very properly, like I said, I'm Todd Underwood. Glad to meet you!"

The two men shook hands, and as they were, Todd added, "Well, Gary! From the feel of that hand shake, it feels like you've been using those weights, quite a bit!"

"Hey thanks! I appreciate that, I really do. Yeah, I've been lifting some for about four or fives years now. I've got two older brothers, Jack, he's 27 and Bobby, he's aged 29, so I kind of inherited their old weights. So whenever I'm home here, I use them, and of course while I'm up at State, I use the weights up there."

"So you got two older brothers, 27 and 29? How old are you? You must be kind of quite a bit younger, right?"

"Yeah, I'm only 21, but got two older sisters between me and the guys. Vicki, she's 23 and Patty, she's 26. So I'm not a late arrival, just the last one in the line of five. But with the two big bruising older brothers though, I found out real early I needed to use the weights and beef myself up if I was gonna survive being around them! They don't have any pity on their little baby brother, let me tell you!"

"Shit man. If you call them the two big bruising brothers, how big are they? They bigger than you?"

"Yeah, yeah they are! I'm like six foot one, and about 190, 95, pounds, and Jack, he's about an inch taller and about 15 pounds heavier – and all solid, I might add! And then there's big Bobby. He's the oldest and the biggest. Six foot three and at least 240, of all man! Yeah, I will admit, all my working out is just trying to look like that bruiser does. I'm not ashamed to admit, he is what his little baby brother wants to look like some day!"

"Well, Gary, I personally think maybe you are on the right road to do that! You look good man, really good!"

"Hey thanks! Really, thanks! It always means a lot to me when another guy has got the guts to tell me I'm looking good! Guys are always so damned afraid to complement another guy for fear everybody's gonna think he's gay or some kind of a fairy guy! Thanks a lot, I appreciate you!"

"Hey man, if one man can't be nice to another guy, this world is in a terrible mess. Yeah – you look good, and I sure am not ashamed to tell you so."

"Hey complements back at you man! You're obviously a little older than me, but you're looking pretty good yourself. You into athletics or something?"

"Yeah Gary, I'm a little older than you. I guess I, and your oldest brother, are the same age, and yeah, I still do some basketball, baseball and jogging, whenever possible, to try 'n stay as hot looking as you younger guys do."

"You 29? You the same age as Bobby?"

"Yeah, I guess so. I'm 29 so if he's 29, then we're the same age. Why? Why you ask?"

"Well, shit man! I always thought Bobby looked good for his age, but shit man, you don't look like you should be more than a year of two older than me!"

"Well, thanks man! Thanks! I do accept that as a complement! Thanks!"

"Wow! Seriously man, I'm shocked. Hey, I've got to level with you! I saw you here the other day, and I thought then that you were somebody about my age, and yeah – I will admit it, I kind of made things work out so that Mom and Dad would be gone this afternoon just so that I had to be here to let you in. I don't have many friends around here since all my friends left town after high school, so I was kind of hoping maybe I could get to know you a little if we met, and maybe find me a new friend. Had no idea you were as old as you say you are."

"Hey, I sure do appreciate the fact that you did think I was so much younger, but now that we've got that all cleared up, what makes you think we couldn't be friends anyway?"

"Oh hey man! I'm only 21, a college kid, you're 29, probably married and three kids at home. Married guys just don't have the time to hang with us single guys!"

"Hey Gary, look! No wedding ring! No wifey and no kids! Yeah I've got a girlfriend, Julie, but it's just a girlfriend. I don't see why you and I can't be friends and do stuff together if we want! Yeah, age 29 is an old fart to a young kid like you, but it happens to all of us. Hey man, I'd better get this stuff done, since that's why I'm here, don't you think?"

"Yeah I guess so! Is that the piece of carpet you needed for in that closet?"

"Yeah, I told your Mom that I did not want to put in pieced together stuff, so I told her I'd bring in a full piece so it's done right. Got a few places where I want to be sure everything fit right and is fixed down good, and that's about all I've got to do. Won't take me too long."

"OK, I'll be in the basement doing some more lifting. Come on down when you get done, OK?"

"OK will do! Won't take me too long, then I'll be down."

Todd proceeded to fit the additional piece of carpeting into the closet and checked all of the spots that he wanted to make sure had been taken care of correctly. As he finished, he put his tools by the front door, and then went down to the basement where he knew Gary was lifting the weights.

As Todd came down the steps, he heard Gary yell out, "In here Todd, in here!"

Todd turned toward the sound of Gary's voice and found Gary lying on the bench press, totally naked, doing reps with a 175 pound barbell.

As Todd came into the room, Gary placed the bar on the rack, looked at Todd, and noticed that Todd was all eyeballs on Gary's nice soft, five incher that was lying off to the side.

Gary raised his head from the bench, looked at Todd and said, "Hey man! Like I told you upstairs, I like to lift in the nude whenever possible. When on campus at State, can't do it there, so hope it's OK if I do it here. OK?"

"Well, of course man! I mean, it is your house! You can do whatever you want, sure not up to me to say. But – I've gotta to ask! How fucking big does that thing get? Holly mackerel! It's soft and hanging there like some fucking clothes line!"

With that comment and realizing that Todd was totally interested in his dick, and just how big it gets, did start Gary onto the road of getting hard. Suddenly it quit just laying there and started to straighten itself out."

"Oh shit! Maybe I'd better put some shorts on! You talking about it is kind of making it get hard."

"Hey man, don't put shorts on for me! Let it do its thing!"

"Hey man, it's getting harder and harder. I'm not so sure I should just let it keep getting bigger and bigger, should I?"

"I don't know – I don't know. That's kinda up to you! Sure as hell ain't bothering me any. Bothering you? This off base for you? Ever have some other guy watch it get hard?"

"Yeah, yeah – yeah sometimes." Gary very softly and shyly answered. "Yeah – sometimes."

"Gary, you play around with guys? You play with guys?"

"Oh God yeah – yeah I do. Please don't be pissed at me or get mad. Yeah, I do. When I saw you the other day I really wanted to see you all naked and I kind of got all carried away with thinking maybe I could play with you, but man, maybe I'm wrong! Todd I just never even thought about maybe you being a straight guy. I just got so all wrapped up in they idea of wanting to play with you, I just never considered that maybe you're not gay. Hey, I'm sorry! Yeah, I kind of got this all set up once I found out you had to come back. Man, I gotta admit, I was really hoping maybe you played with guys too. Hey man, when you came to the front door, I knew as soon as you got out of your truck it was you. I was watching to make sure it was you and to make sure nobody was with you. I had other clothes laying there if I had to use them. I think you are one hot guy and yeah – I was hoping maybe – just maybe. Hey – please don't tell anybody! Please! I just let myself get all out of control. I'm sorry, man, I'm sorry!"

"Look at that dick of yours! God man, it must be at least nine inches long, right? My God – I've never seen a dick that big before!"

"Hey Todd, let me grab some shorts man, let me get something on! I think I was really way off base here, I think I really goofed! I'm sorry! Let me get up from here and get some shorts! I goofed man, and now I'm feeling really stupid and funny!"

"Hey – it's just you and me in the house? Right?"

"Yeah, of course or I won't have been laying all naked like this! Why?"

"How much time till somebody comes home?"

"Well, I know Mom and Dad aren't coming home till after having dinner with some friends, so – why? Are you – maybe – are you – oh Todd!"

Just as Gary asked again, "Oh, are you – oh are you – oh," that is when Todd stepped his right leg up and over the hot looking, prone naked body of Gary, bent over, opened his mouth widely, and with his left hand guiding its direction, Todd let Gary know that what he had expressed his desires to be, were quickly and without asking, becoming a reality.

"Oh my God man – oh my God!" Gary quickly and emphatically said, as he grabbed the sides of Todd's head and fed all of his nine-inch rod, deep into Todd's mouth!

"Oh I can't believe this. Oh man I was so sure I had really goofed up once I let you see my dick. Oh man the whole time you were here in the house I was just so fucking sure that what I was doing was OK, then when you came in here and I was all naked, then I thought I had really screwed up bad! Oh Todd! Oh, thank God man you understand me. Oh yeah, yeah! Oh you are so hot to me! Yeah suck on me, please!"

Todd bent over and enjoyed the feel of Gary's nine inches filling the inside of his mouth and his throat and then stood up and started to pull his shirt off.

"OK? OK if I do this?" Todd asked as he started to undress, still straddling across the bench and Gary, combined.

"Oh yeah man, yeah! Yeah, get naked too! I wanna see you all naked! All bare and all naked man!"

After removing all of his clothing, including his tight while briefs that he had on, since when he left the house earlier, he did not have even one small hint in his mind that he would be stripping down in front of anybody, let alone one hot hunky younger athletic man. As Todd finished taking off his Levi's, he once again stepped his right leg up and over the bench and Gary, and then moved up toward Gary's face and offered him his stick of male excitement.

"Here man, you suck? Want some of me?"

"Oh yes, oh yes – oh yeah fuck my face man – fuck my face!"

Todd moved in for the ram, and he did that exactly – he grabbed ahold of Gary's head, pulled it forward, and he rammed Gary's face with his dick.

"Oh, suck me man, suck me! Seriously man, you are not going to believe this, but you are only the second guy to ever have my dick in his mouth! This is only the second time I've ever done this with some guy. Your big fucking dick is the only the second one I've ever touched, other than the guy that I played with earlier this week! Seriously man, this is just time number two for me. Thank God I did that stuff earlier with David or I'm not sure what I would have done when I came in here and found you laying there all naked. And shit, especially with the size of a dick you've got! Oh, thank goodness you did this and thank goodness I was ready for it! Hey man. Just don't let my boss know I did this with one of his customers. Oh man – yeah suck on that dick! Suck on that dick!"

With Todd firmly positioned directly above Gary's face, with his dick rammed completely and fully down into Gary's mouth, Todd used the barbell, resting on the rack, as his handhold as he raised and lowered himself into and back out of Gary's mouth.

Switching back and forth a number of times, well, rather a great number of times, Todd would fuck Gary's face, then pull off and move down to where Gary could fuck Todd's face, or another way of looking at it is – Todd's mouth fucked Gary's stiff dick.

Gary looked at Todd and said, "Hey, let's go into my bedroom and get in bed together? Can we?"

"Well, yeah, I guess so, if you think we can. Your bedroom down here? You sure nobody'll be coming home?"

"Yeah, Mom and Dad are gone all day! Oh, I want to fuck your ass! Can I please? Please?"

"Yeah man, if you know it's OK. Sure, I'd love to feel that big dick of yours up in my ass. Yeah, let's go do it!"

Gary led Todd out of the area where the weights were and led him into his bedroom, there in the basement of the house. Both men were obviously already naked from their weight room playing, and they immediately hit the bed.

"Hey man, you want me on my back or on my gut? Which way you wanta fuck me?"

"Hey let me hold your legs up and fuck you on your back. I want to watch your face while I fuck your butt. OK? That OK?"

"Oh yeah, man, yeah, that's OK. Just fuck the hell out of me! Like I just told you, thank goodness I did this just a few days ago or I'd be real afraid of letting you push that thing up in me. Hey – like they say, you do it once, you want it every day! I sure as hell never expected this to happen when I came over here today. Fuck me man! Let me feel that big nine inches up in me!"

After smearing some grease on his dick and also on Todd's ass, Gary grabbed Todd's leg, pushed them up in the air so he had a good eyesight of Todd's tight butt hole – he aimed his dick and said, "I'm coming in man, I'm coming in! Ready to take me? Ready?"

"Oh God yes, God yes! Yeah, let me feel it! Push it in me! Fuck me!"

Using all the good motions one man can use on another man when fucking the hell out of his ass, Gary used Todd's butt hole as strongly and as forcefully as he could for fifteen or twenty minutes.

"Oh man, you have one hot ass man, one hot ass! You feel good! How you feeling? Want to fuck me some? I could use some dick like yours up in my ass!"

"Oh yeah man – yeah! I've never fucked some guy's ass yet. I told you that I've only played around with a guy once, and that was just a few nights ago. I never fucked him! That was my very first time getting together with a guy, and he taught me how to suck and get sucked off, and he fucked me with his dick and some dildos he has, but we never got around to me fucking his ass. Yeah Gary, yeah, can I fuck you?"

"Hell yeah man! Hell yeah! I like this! I get to be your first piece of ass to fuck! I like that! Hey, I'm gonna lay down on my gut so you can lay on top of me and figure out what you're doing back there, OK?"

"Yeah, yeah! Oh man, I can't believe this! The other night I never even thought about fucking his ass. Hell man – I don't even think we had enough time for me to do that too. Oh man, he used some of the biggest fucking dildos on my ass! He sure as hell showed me I love to get my ass fucked and played with! Thank goodness we did that the other night or I'd been too afraid to let you put that big thing of yours up in me. Hey, anything special I need to know before I poke you and this pretty little ass of yours?"

"No, not really. If you got fucked and had some dildos used on you the other night, then I assume you already know that you need to go in pretty slow until you get my butt hole opened up, right? I want you up in there, but just make sure I'm open and ready for it before you get too wild. OK?"

"Yeah got it man, got it! Oh, I'm gonna fuck you! Oh man, what a trip! You feel me? You feel my dick? I'm going in!"

"Yeah, I feel it. Go slow for a minute. Yeah, that's right, yeah! Oh yeah, oh yeah, I just felt you go in! OK, you're in! You're in! Yeah – push man, yeah – push! Yeah, let's do it! Do it! Fuck me man, fuck me hard! You're fucking a guy's ass yeah – fuck it good!"

Todd did not need to be asked more than once to fuck him hard. He heard the instruction and he followed suit!

"Oh God yes, yeah, God yes! Oh man your ass feels so fucking good! Oh man it's so tight on my dick! It feels so good grabbing my ass. Oh man, are you squeezing it with your ass? Oh yeah, I can feel that! Yeah I can tell you're doing that with your ass aren't you? Oh yeah man, oh yeah! Oh yeah, feels like some kind of pliers on it and grabbing it! Oh man that feels so fucking good! Oh man, oh – I'm about to cum man, I'm about to cum!! I gotta cum man, I gotta cummmmm! Can I cum in your ass? Can I cum in your ass?"

"Yeah man, yeah! Let it fly, let me feel it! Yeah – oh yeah I can feel you loading my ass! Oh, tell me! How you like loading a guy's ass? Oh man – oh man, that feels good!"

Then with a laugh in his voice, Gary added. "Oh shit man, for a fucking old, 29 year old, you sure can shoot the cum shots, can't you?"

"Oh shit man, I'm fucking exhausted man! Gary, I am fucking exhausted! Hey man, not sure if it's the 29 years old thing or that fucking hot and tight ass of yours, but shit man, what a great feeling I got right now! Oh, between you and David, the guy I played with the other night, I can't believe what in the hell I've gotten to do, what I've had done to me, and gotten to feel this week! Oh – I am now a totally different person now than I was a few days ago! Oh – yeah, man – let's do be friends! Let's be real close friends! Thanks for letting me fuck you, thank you man! Thank you! I love this! You are one hot fucker man, you really are!"

CHAPTER SEVEN:

In Apartment 224

"Joe, take the truck back to the warehouse and get it loaded for tomorrow. I've got to check out this west wing of these apartments and see what we need to order, and I'll call and have somebody come pick me up – whenever I'm done. I have no idea right now how many units need to be looked at, nor how long it's gonna take, so I'll just call when I'm about done and have you or someone come and get me."

Having given Joe, his helper, the game plan for the rest of the afternoon, Todd grabbed his clip board, the master key for the apartments, his measuring tape and a few other items that he knew he would need, and sent Joe on his way.

The North Cove Apartment complex was a new project for the carpet company. It was an older set of apartments, about 80 or more in total, and the carpet store that Todd installed for had won the bid to take over the carpet and tile maintenance, under a contract agreement. This was Todd's first occasion to visit the complex and determine just what was necessary at this particular time.

Checking his "vacant apartment" sheet, Todd measured and checked out probably 10 or twelve apartments when suddenly he realized that he was being watched by somebody in the apartment across the hall.   The door was standing open, but Todd did not remember it being open when he was looking for apartment number 223.

Looking over toward the common hall, Todd saw and nodded to a rather quite attractive man, about age 40, 41 or so, that was very interested in watching, apparently, every move Todd made.

As Todd nodded to him, the man came out of his apartment and came across the hall to where Todd was down on his hands and knees measuring a small offset area.

As the man came into the apartment, he said, "Hi, I'm Mark. I live across the hall over in 224. You the new maintenance man?"

Todd rather sat up, kneeling on his knees and setting back on his heals, extended his hand out for a hand shake and replied, "Well, no! I'm not the maintenance man. I work for the carpet and tile company that will be taking care of the flooring. We just took over the contract, so I'm here getting some measurements and finding out which apartments are needing some attention. I'm Todd Underwood."

As Todd spoke, he noticed that his new acquaintance was making no effort to step back any. Having reached out his hand for a friendly hand shake, had rather dictated that the man step up close, to reach Todd's hand. Now that they were done shaking hands, Todd realized that this man's crotch was still placed very, very, closely right in front of his face. Not a real unpleasant situation for Todd, but he did think it was rather unusual since it was now forcing Todd to strain looking so directly up, to talk to the man.

"Need something to drink? Kind of hot in here ain't it?" Mark asked, as he looked so directly down at Todd, still kneeling on the floor in front of him.

Multitudes of questions and comments were suddenly running through Todd's head. "Why is he standing so close to my face? Why did he come over here? Is he OK or is he acting a little weird? Is he built like I think he is from what I can see from down here? Is his crotch kind of standing out a little more than it did at first? God, does he smell as good as I think he does? Shit man, is he kinda smacking and licking his lips when he looks down at me? God, look at those legs! Stacks of steel! Oh man, his crotch is getting bigger and bigger,

I know it is! Damn I wish he was standing back a little so I could just look at his crotch and not have him know it. Oh shit man, is he, yeah he is – he's touching his dick! Oh man he's sliding his finger over his dick! Oh shit man, I know damn well it's getting bigger and bigger! Oh shit man, he's actually making his dick get bigger and bigger just standing there! Oh man, is he trying to come on to me? Oh man, would I do it with him – oh hell yes, I would! He is a fucking hot looking man, fucking hot!"

As Todd finally failed to keep his eyes off of Mark's large protruding basket, (against all of his attempts to keep himself under control), Mark again so slightly slid his finger across it, and Todd replied, "Hot – oh yeah, yeah, it is, isn't it? Yeah, you have something? If you do, I'd appreciate it!"

"Yeah, I've got some coke and some lemon lime stuff. Which you prefer?"

"Oh hey the coke sounds pretty refreshing to me right now. That would be great!"

"OK come on. It's in the frig, over at my place. This damn apartment is too damn hot to stay in, anyway! Cooler's on over at my place." And having said that, Mark reached down and after placing his hands under each of Todd's arm pits, he lifted him up from the floor as if he was taking care of some small child.

Todd was stunned and somewhat shocked, but at the same time, horny as hell and confused, not wanting to do or say anything – if there was something headed his way with this hunk – but at the same time, not really knowing if playing his hand was really the right thing to do. Was this hunk actually trying to set things up, or was Todd starting to loose reality, just because this guy was looking very, very delightful, and was suddenly making Todd once again, realize that he was now much more anxious to see some hot and hunky guy, especially one that is hardly dressed or covered up, than to see some almost naked gal that is trying to show everything to everybody!

Stunned and rather shook at the aspect of actually being picked up from the floor, Todd stood face to face with Mark and each man looked directly into the eyes of his, now, face to face, acquaintance. Todd said nothing, but he did, silently and completely, admire the return look and the solid facial expression coming back to him, from what he was suddenly realizing was probably the most beautiful man within miles and miles.

As he stood there, completely mesmerized, all Todd could mentally process was: "Oh – what a beautiful face, what a beautiful smile, what a beautiful expression, what a beautiful body, what beautiful eyes, what beautiful legs, what a beautiful, beautiful crotch, oh yes – oh, what a beautiful crotch! It had felt like hours, that he had been kneeling down on the floor, with that gorgeous, beautiful, crotch directly in front of his face – although he had felt so terribly restricted from looking directly at it! He knew he had failed in keeping his eyes from going directly at it, and he knew this hunk of a man had seen him look directly at it, especially since Mark had so lovingly slid his fingers across it, as Todd admired it so closely. Now as he stood there, merely within inches of this man's beautiful face and his grinning smile, he wondered if he dare reach out and just put that enormous bulge of a crotch, in his hand. Oh how he wanted to! He wanted to feel it and squeeze it so badly, but yet did not know if he was starting to 'just loose it" over what was there, or was this really a possible, 'man meets man' situation that he just did not yet have confirmed. Oh he wanted this statue of a man to just throw him down on the floor and just rape him there on the spot! He needed to know for sure, if something this good, actually would do something with him. Todd wanted to just yell, "Rape me, rape me! Fuck me please! Do me! Please let me know you will do me!"

"Hey, it's hot in here. Let's go get that coke for you and help you cool down some." Mark firmly stated, as he turned toward the door and Todd rather numbly, followed.

As Mark walked toward the door and Todd was following behind, Todd simply could not believe what he was being asked to follow, nor what he was actually doing – following that hunk over, and into his own apartment. As Todd admired and attempted to accept the sight walking in front of him, he could not fail to register, that beautiful, beautiful sight, deep into his brain!

As Todd attempted to walk without falling all over his companion, Todd kept running through his mind: 'Six foot one or two, neck that has to be at least 17 or 18 inches around, a back shaped like the "Y" of two roads taking off in two different directions, a waist that is smaller than my own, and sitting right up on top of two butt muscles that are simply droplets of solid gold! Oh God he is so hot! He is so fucking hot!'

With each step, Todd could watch Mark's butt muscles move and contract, tighten and loosen, only so very slightly hidden under the very thin, light weight, actually see-through, cotton shorts that Mark had on – well almost had on. So tight, so short, so thin, so showing of everything he had inside, that Todd actually wondered why he had any shorts on at all. The shorts actually showed his dick visually and shape wise! "What a tease! Oh man, what a tease! Oh if I'm wrong about this man, I'm in deep shit and trouble! Oh man, no straight guy can look this hot to another man, can he?"

As they entered apartment 224, Mark stepped aside, so that Todd could step in front of himself, and he then closed the door.

"Hey, let's keep the cool air in here as much as possible, OK?" Mark stated as he closed the door, and immediately threw both arms around Todd and pulled him close for a full, powerful, deep throated kiss!

Todd was shocked! Actually more than shocked! He was stunned, flabbergasted and more than bowled over, in attempting to realize, of just what was happening. He knew his dreams of a few minutes ago were now coming true. He knew this hunk of a man was not some mirage. He knew, he could feel him, and that he was real. And, this man of unbelievable sight was starting to make serious, serious love to him. He knew he had not done anything to make this happen, so he knew this man, of magazine picture status and quality, was in complete control.

"Oh Todd! Oh, I've wondered what your name was for weeks now! Oh Todd, I've wanted to grab you and hug you and kiss you like this ever since the very first time I saw you! You are such a cutie man, a real cutie! Oh Todd, I am so glad this has finally happened! It has taken way too long! Hey man, get stripped, I want you naked and I want you in my bed with me, and I want it now! I've wanted that ass of yours since the very first time I saw it! Damn it looks tight and hard!"

Still gripped tightly with Mark's enormous arms around him, and with Mark's now very excited crotch being pressed up against him, which was making his own dick grow, Todd attempted to ask. "Mark, wait! What do you mean ever since the first time you saw me? When? Where? Mark, this it the first time I've been here. I've never been here before! What do you mean?"

"Hey honey, down at the Boot and Belt Bar! Man, I have drooled over you for months in there, but with Bobby with me, I had to just let it go! When I saw you in here today, man I knew it was finally my time to let me tell you how fucking hot I have always thought you were, and I will admit, I shed my clothes as fast as I could, just so I could let you get an early, easy, sight, at the major hardon you give me! Oh Todd, come on, let's go in here and let me roam that hot bod of yours. Come on! I want to feel you man, come on!"

Still being gripped tightly, Todd was now trying to pull his head back a little farther and ask, "Mark – the Boot and Belt Bar? Where is that? I've never been there! What are you talking about?"

Suddenly Mark let loose of Todd, stepped back, looked sternly at Todd and said, "Todd, the Levi Leather bar over on Second Street. I see you in there all the time. You're always there by yourself, but Bobby is always with me, so I've never gotten to meet you. Well, – that is until today! I've asked around some, and everybody said they thought you were single, and when I found that out, it just made me that much more horny for you! Come on man, get stripped, I want some of you!"

"Mark, I've never been in a Levi Leather bar! I don't even know where it's at. That's not me! I've never been there!"

"Oh come on man, you're the guy I see in there like every Saturday night, right? You are that guy – aren't you?"

Rather uncomfortably the two men stood close to each other, but no longer hugging as they had been just a few minutes ago.

"No, no, I'm not that guy! I'm sorry but no, I'm not that guy! I don't even know where that bar is. I've never been in a Levi Leather type of bar."

"Oh God man, Todd, I am so sorry! Oh man, I must have really screwed up this time! Oh Todd, really, I thought you were that guy that I see there every Saturday night. Todd, you don't drive a red Mustang? Really, that's not you?"

"No Mark, it's not me, but let's not get ourselves all out of shape here! Everything is OK, really it is! Everything is OK! Believe me man, it is!"

"Oh man! I've never screwed up this way before at all! Really I never have! I am so sorry! Yeah man, I thought you were that guy and I wanted to play with you. Oh God, I am so sorry! Please forgive me, please forgive me. Hey, don't think all gay guys are this messed up man, please don't think they're all like this! I'm sorry!"

"Whoa, man whoa! Hey man, let's talk here! Don't get all upset, slow down! I'm not the guy you thought I was, but right now I'm glad! You hugging me and giving me that kiss, it is by far the best damn thing that has happened to me for days! I probably want you more than you want me. I've only had a couple of times with guys, but I'm learning, and please – I want to play. Can we? I know I'm the wrong guy, but please man, you are so fucking hot to me that I sure don't want to walk out of here now! No way, man, no way! Please, please! Just a few days ago, before I finally got together with a guy, and then found out what gay sex is really like, then I might not have been so anxious, but now – please – please! I want to, and I need to have sex with you!"

Mark rather stood there and looked at Todd with a look of bewilderment and confusion on his face, and Todd then finally reached out and grabbed the hot looking, protruding crotch that had so recently been directly in front of his face. "Please Mark, please," Todd pleaded as he slid his fingers under the elastic waist band, of the very showy, sexy, hot, shorts, and started to pull them down.

Continuing to look at Mark's face, and pleading for some type of an OK from him, Todd continued to slide the firm hugging shorts on down, and allowed Mark's stiffened rod to come flying out, and just almost hit him in the face. Looking at it from only about three or four inches away, Todd looked up toward Mark's face and saw the man looking back down with ever so slightly of a grin on his face. Todd accepted that, in fact he would have accepted anything right then, as his signal to take that rod and eat it!

Mark stepped out of his, now on the floor, shorts and placed his hands on Todd's head. "Oh yeah man, oh yeah! Yeah suck it man, suck it! That feels good!"

Standing in his kitchen, Mark was now getting sucked off by some younger man, that he thought just so slightly earlier, that he knew who he was, but now had found out he had played up to the wrong guy. Shaking his head slightly as if mystified, Mark was enjoying the mouth action on his dick, and at the same time wondering if this should be happening at all.

"Hey Todd, hey you did tell me your name is Todd, right? I feel so confused right now. Todd, stand up here a minute. I really did think you were that other guy from the bar. You must have a twin in town man, really, the two of you are identical. I don't go after guys that I don't know, and I'm feeling kind of funny here having you sucking on me when I really don't even know you or anything about you! I guess you must be gay, well anyway, especially since you've been sucking on my dick, right?"

Todd sternly looked at Mark and said, "Hey, my man! Hey, don't get all freaked out just cause you thought I was some other guy. Man, if you thought he was that hot, and now you are telling me, he and I should be twins, I'm taking that as a pretty good complement! Yeah, I'm gay! Well, – anyway, I guess I'm in the process of deciding I am. Really, I've only had gay sex for about three or four times now, but let me tell you man, when you came into that apartment and walked up so close to me with that beautiful basket sticking right at my face, I knew damn well right then that I was gonna have some sex before I left this building – even if I had to grab you and throw you down to do it. I've been taught some pretty good stuff in the few times that I've played with guys, and I want you to teach me some more! OK? Yeah, I'm the wrong guy, but let's just take this as one great experience that I sure never expected to happen today, and I guess neither did you!

Hey, since you were gonna do the other guy this afternoon, then I have to assume you've got the time to do me instead, right? I mean, that Bobby guy you mentioned. Is he your lover? Will he be coming home or something? Is it a problem that I'm here?"

"No, hell no! I mean it's no problem that you're here! And that Bobby, no he's not my lover, just a close friend! Hey man, I kind of screwed up in thinking you were the other guy, but – so be it! Maybe this is better. I guess you don't have a lover since you told me you've only done the guy thing a few times, right?"

"Right! I do have a girl friend, well let's say, right now, I have a girl friend, but, I tried screwing her the other night, and the whole damn time I was on her, all I could do was wish she was one of the guys, that I've played with. I damn near couldn't even get a hardon with her. I think those days are really numbered. Not so sure how I'm gonna break off an eight year relationship without telling her she needs a dick, but, guess I'll have to figure out something. So – now that you kinda know my situation, can I strip off and let both of us be standing here bare assed naked and let me get to you and that dick of yours again? Seriously man, I want to fuck around with you, I want to suck on that dick of yours again, and I want us to play! I'd love to watch you suck on my dick! I want to feel your mouth on it! Please?"

"Come on Todd, let's go in the bedroom. Let's get you all stripped down and naked and let me – as you say – 'fuck around with you.' What do you like to do? What activities have you done since you got started in the, more fun ways of, having sex? You been fucked in the ass yet?"

As they moved into the bedroom from the kitchen area, Mark was asking the questions, and Todd was in the process of unbuttoning and unbuckling everything necessary so that he could dump his clothes just as soon as possible. He was following one hell of a hot, masculine sturdy body from the kitchen and he wanted to be ready to either grab it, or have it grab him when they got into the bedroom.

"Oh yeah, yeah I have been, and I found out, well anyway I was told, I have one really hungry asshole. David, the guy that I did stuff with the first time, well, he has some dildos, and he used some of them on me. One of them was a big one! He kept telling me I was doing good taking it, but I will tell you, it felt like it was gonna rip me apart going in. David kept telling me that the way I like to have my ass stuffed with big stuff, that he just knows I'm the kind of a guy that will be getting fisted pretty soon. He said my ass needs big stuff up in it to make it happy! So, since he's the experienced guy, and I'm the learner, I have to assume he must know what he's talking about, right?"

Reaching out toward Todd, Mark said, "Come on, come on, let me at you! Here, let me help you get those pants off. I want to see just what size dick you've got in there! I need to chew me some dick. Shit man, I really fucked up thinking you were that other guy from the bar, but right now, I'm fucking glad I did! You are one hot looking young man! Holy crap man! Look at that dick! Oh man alive, feed me – come on man, feed me!"

Todd certainly did not need any additional requests to stick his dick in Mark's mouth and get it sucked on! He got all of his clothes off and out of the way, and as Mark laid down on the bed and had Todd stand there, right in front of his mouth, Mark reached out, grabbed Todd by the hips and pulled him forward. Mark's mouth open, Todd's dick hard, and all the way in, immediately! With Todd pushing forward, and Mark pulling Todd's body toward his face, Todd's dick went in fast and hard! All the way!

"Oh yeah man, oh yeah! Oh man please suck me and bite me! Oh yeah! Please suck me hard! Eat my dick! Bite me! Let me feel your teeth on my dick! Oh yeah, reach up here and pinch my tits please! Yeah, harder man, harder! Oh I love this! Oh yeah man, oh yeah! Eat my dick, eat my dick!"

As Todd stood beside the bed, he jerked his body back and forth and he fed his hard ramming dick into Mark's mouth, and continued to beg for Mark to pinch his tits harder and harder! Pinch me hard! Make me yell! Yeah man, I love rough sex man, I love it! Yeah man I love that! I love that! Todd grabbed Mark's head and pulled him onto his dick as far as possible and for five or six minutes, a person in an adjoining apartment could have thought there might be an earthquake happening with the amount of shaking going on in that bedroom! Todd was using Mark's mouth, and Mark's mouth was using Todd's dick, and the shaking was strong!

All of a sudden, Todd threw his head up toward the ceiling and actually yelled out loud, "Yeah man! Yeah! Oh yes! Do me, do me!" and just as he let out the "Do me, do me," he dumped his thick, warm, man, cream load, down and into Mark's mouth!

"Oh man, oh man, oh man! Oh shit I didn't know I was gonna cum that fast! Oh shit man, I shot! God, right now I feel like I shot a cannon full! Oh man, oh man, I'm exhausted! Oh Mark, I gotta lay down! Let me lay beside you!"

"Hey guy! Hey, before you lay down here, hand me that rag over there on the bed stand. Man you shot so much cum at me and into me so fast, I've still got part of it running down my chin. God man! Ain't you shot off for a month or more? Wow! What a mouth full! Tastes good though? Just did not expect so much, so fast! Guess I can understand now why you really didn't care if I got you all mixed up with that other guy or not. You were fucking ready for some good shooting, weren't you?"

"Yeah I was! I knew I was, but I will admit I sure didn't expect it to fly so fucking fast! Man, when that happens, it pisses me off cause that means the sucking is over. Well, for a little while anyway! Oh man – your mouth felt so fucking good on my dick! Oh that felt good!"

"Well, you know what guy! You just told me that your other friend told you that you have one hungry ass and it likes to have stuff stuffed up in it, right?"

"Yeah, yeah right! David stuck some pretty big dildos up in my butt that night, so yeah, I guess my ass is kind of a hungry hole! You gonna fill it for me? Please?"

"Yeah, I'm gonna fill it! Don't know if I'm gonna fill it with as much load as you just gave me, but I do know one thing, I'm gonna have some good fun getting my dick all ready to give you whatever it's got. Roll over here. Give me that ass! God, what a beautiful tight little ass! Man, right now, that thing sure don't look like it's ever had anything put up in there!"

After putting just a little amount of ass lube jelly on his dick, Mark threw his leg over Todd's back and without hardly any time spent on aiming his eight inch long, and about six inch around rod, he immediately went into Todd's ass the whole way.

"Todd let out a scream of, "Ouch! Oh God! Oh God that hurt man! Oh shit! Oh man that hurt! Oh man when you pushed in like that it hurt like hell! Oh God, my ass!"

"Hey lay there! Yeah, lay there! You're OK! Just lay there! I knew it was gonna be kind of sharp slamming it in that way, but you already told me you like rough sex, and man, there ain't no place better to have rough sex than back there in your ass! See, don't hurt now does it? See, only hurts for a second, don't it? Todd, you told me your buddy said you've got the kind of an ass that's getting ready to be fisted! That little punch ain't nothing to what you'll feel when you get a fist slammed up in there. Believe me man, when that happens, this little pain will be nothing, believe me, nothing!"

"Mark – do you get fisted? Do you?"

"Yeah man, yeah! As often as possible!"

"Oh man I'm about afraid to ask. Do you fist other guys? Do you do fisting?"

"Hell yeah man! Hell yeah. If a guy's gonna take a fist up his own ass, he better know how to stick his fist up in some other guy's ass! Why you wanting to know? Why you asking? You kinda getting turned on talking, or thinking, about maybe getting a fist put up in your ass? That idea getting you all hot 'n bothered?"

"I don't know, I don't know! I never talked to a guy before about getting a fist put up his ass, or putting his fist up in another guy's ass. Yeah, yeah I guess it is kind of exciting to me. Yeah, I guess so! Yeah – it's making me breath real heavy right now! Yeah, I guess that is turning me on, isn't it? Oh man something is! Yeah man, the way I feel right now, yeah it sure is! Really I don't know if it's that talking about fisting, you ramming that big thick dick of yours up in my butt, just you laying on top of me or me just getting to feel you and your body all naked against mine or what, but hell yes man, I'm really fucking turned on! I've never been this fucking excited for sex before. Even the very first time I ever fucked around, I was never this fucking turned on and hot for it!"

"Good man! Good! I like a guy in bed that's turned on! That's good. That's good for sex! You OK now? Ready to really get that little butt of yours fucked and fucked good and hard?"

"Yeah, I'm OK now. I'm sorry I yelled! I'm sorry. It don't hurt any more now. I should have just gritted my teeth and kept quiet. I'm sorry! I'm sorry!" And Todd then continued, "Fuck me man, please fuck me!"

"No problem man! I knew it was gonna happen. My dick ain't the skinniest one around, and when it goes in all of a sudden, it has to force that tight little asshole of yours open. That sure ain't the first time I made some guy scream when I poked it in him and up in his little ass! The dick is good and stiff, and good and hard, so it sure ain't gonna give any. That just means the little hole it's going into is the thing that has got to give. Sorry about the hurt, but man, you took it, and I'm proud! You're my kind of a man!"

"So I guess maybe you kind of like rougher sex too – right? You like to really get to it, don't you? You did great pinching my tits. You pinched them harder than I've been able to get any of the other guys to pinch 'em. I like the way you went after 'em. That felt good!"

"Good! Good! Glad to hear that! How's this dick feeling up in your ass now? Feeling better?"

"Oh yeah man, it's feeling good! Real good! Pound me! Pound my ass! Yeah do it hard! Real hard!! Slam it man, yeah, slam it! Make me squeal man, make me squeal! I like it – yeah man – yeah I like it! Pound it, pound it! Oh man, you've got me so hot and ready, I'll do anything now! Pound my ass! Drill me with that big rod of yours! Slam that fucker in me, and slam it in good! Slam it in me! Do me! Do me!"

"Hang on kid, hang on! I'm not sure just how hard you've been pounded back here before, but I've got to admit it's been some time since I've had me some nice fresh beef in my bed that's asking for it like you are, so I'm gonna do you like I wish I could every guy! God, oh God! I love this, I love this! Oh Todd, your ass is gonna be black and blue when I get done back here! Hang on man! I'm fucking you like I ain't fucked any guy for one hell of a long time! God this is hot man – this is fucking hot!"

Todd was spread eagle across the bed with his hands extended out and up, and of course his legs spread apart with Mark laying in his butt, and literally beating the hell out of his ass. Mark's slamming up and down and using that good tight ass to its fullest, was making Todd jerk up and down on the bed. Todd's head and arms kept flying up and down each time Mark once again pulled up and then slammed back down into him.

"Do me, do me, do me!" Was just about all that Todd could manage to get out of his mouth. Even though he wanted to tell Mark that this was better than just 'great' to him, the way his body was being slammed up and down on the mattress, he simply couldn't speak! Every time he attempted to say something, his face slammed back down onto the mattress. All Todd could do, was keep telling himself, "Oh my God, I've got a fucking madman fucking my ass! Oh God he is fucking the hell out of me! Oh fuck man – fuck me man – fuck me! Fuck me hard man, fuck me hard! I love it! Yeah, pound the hell out of my ass Sir, pound me! Yeah do it, do it, do it!"

After a full five minutes of taking this body abuse, although to Todd it certainly would not be called abuse, Mark suddenly grabbed hold of Todd around his chest, and threw his dick into Todd's ass, as far in as he could possibly get it to go! He turned rigid! He was pushing on Todd's ass with everything he had! He hugged Todd to the point to where Todd almost could not catch his breath. Suddenly Mark let out a sudden and surprising, "Ohhhhhhhh, oh man! Oh man, I'm cummmmmmin' man, I'm cummmmmmin'!" Once again for a few quick but very solid and strong strokes, he slammed his rod back into the very depths, of Todd's ass. Todd could tell from inside, this man was actually trying to put his entire body up inside of his ass. Todd felt that he was pushing, with his dick, just about that fucking hard!"

Still trying to get some breath, since he was being held so tightly, Todd tried to say, "Yeah man, yeah! Do it, do it! Cum man, cum man! Shoot man, shoot!"

Then, just as Mark actually collapsed on top of Todd, and he let loose of his tremendous bear hug grip, he dropped his head down beside Todd's, took a big deep breath and softly said, "Oh my God man, I want you! Oh – I want you so bad! Honey – I have not felt like this for years! Babe, I'm off duty for four more days yet and I wanta keep fucking the hell out of you till I have to report back on duty! Everyday man! Everyday! Every hour man! Every hour! Please, we need to do this everyday! This trooper ain't felt this good in years! Oh, I need you man! You better say OK man, or I'm gonna throw the fucking cuffs on you! I need you and I need you badly! My vacation hasn't been shit until now, but man alive, it sure is getting better and better the more I feel your ass! Man, I ain't talked to any player about getting his first fist up in his ass, or helped him get one up in there, for years now! Oh man, this vacation is gonna turn out good! Isn't it? Come on man, tell me it is! Come on man, talk to me!"

CHAPTER EIGHT:

"What Do You Say? Interested?"

Still laying under the hot fucking man that had just pounded the hell out of his ass, and in conclusion, dumped a major, major cum load into his ass, Todd asked, "Mark, Mark! What did you just say? Did you just say trooper and cuffs? Mark, are you an officer?"

"Yeah, guy, yeah! Kind of failed to tell you I guess – you were getting your ass pounded by one of the state's finest! Your cute tight little ass has just been fucked and pounded by one of the guys that all the gay guys are always trying to figure out how to get in bed. Well, Todd my man, you've just been loaded with some of the state's finest juices! And yeah! I do intend to do this often. If you're just getting into the gay stuff, you sure as hell are one fast learner! Seriously, I have not fucked any guy's ass, or beat his body that hard in years, and yet you kept begging for more. You are one hot ass! One hot ass! I can't believe how hard and rough you want it done to you! Man I gotta say, you sure as hell can take it! Man, can you still move?"

"Mark – you're a state trooper? Man, I can't believe this! Yeah, I know! I know all gays are always wanting to make it with a cop. Man, I can't believe this! I've just got the fucking hell of a lifetime, and by a hot fucking state cop! Let me tell you, you sure as hell aren't the only one that wants to do this some more! So do I! Shit man! The way you fucked me and pounded my ass, I could feel you way up inside of me! Yeah man, yeah! I want to do this everyday too!"

Smiling toward Todd, Mark stated, "Seriously man, I can not believe some guy that just got started getting his ass fucked, can take what I just gave you! Size, action and load, all of it! Man, I sure can see why that other guy said your ass is headed for getting fisted pretty damn quick. Shit man, I think if I could have put my fist, and probably more, up in there at the same time I had my dick in there, you'd been yelling 'Thanks." I'm not sure what your limit back here is! I'm not sure you even have a limit back here! Us cops like to think we're the big and tough guys, but I haven't been in any cop's ass yet, that can take what I just gave you!"

"In any cop's ass? Oh shit – do you fuck some of the other cops!? Seriously, do you and some of the other cops fuck each other?"

Still laying there, his dick still stuck up in Todd's ass, although not as far, now that it was starting to deflate, Mark replied. "Yeah man! Yeah! Us cops, we need sex and fucking around just like everybody else. We're all buddies, and when one of us finds out that one of the new guys is into doing the guy thing, well then we kind of just get 'em included into our little ring of gay cops. Cops that do other gay cops! We've got our little groups that we can stop by and visit, all over the state. You let me keep fucking you like I did today, and then maybe we can do ourselves a little out of town tripping, and see if you can take it from some of the other guys as roughly as you took it from me, or maybe, see if a bunch of us together can make you yell Uncle!"

Flipping his head as far as he could, in an attempt to look at Mark's face, Todd excitedly asked, "Oh man! You mean you'd take me to go fuck around with some of the other cops, and maybe let them fuck me too? Oh, is that what you're saying?"

"Yeah sure! Why not? Some of the other guys have brought some playmates with them once in awhile to kind of share with the rest of us, and so sure, why not? If you keep begging for the rough and wild action that you like up in your ass, then maybe we just need to have more than one guy standing by to take over when I get all wiped out!"

"Oh, this is unbelievable! Oh I can't believe this! What – within just about two minutes, I find out that the guy that just fucked the hell out of my ass and has still got his dick up in there, is a State Trooper, and now you're telling me that you'll let me go with you and get fucked by some more cops? Oh, this is way too wild to even think is possible! Oh man, just thinking about that is getting me all fucking excited again. Oh come on man, come on! Fuck me some more? Please, please, please! Would you please?"

"Sure I will, sure! This tight fucking ass of yours, hell yes! Lay still man. Here goes! Hang on!"

Todd did. He spread his arms out like they had been previously, and firmly planed his feet on the edge of the bed, knowing that as soon as Mark raised up just slightly, his ass was going to get rammed and slammed, pushed and crushed, probably even harder than he had been done before.

For ten minutes more, Todd's body laid there and flipped and flopped on the bed as Mark used every bit of his energy and strength in actually trying to get Todd to kind of suggest that he had taken enough. It never happened! But Mark's climax did. Once again, suddenly Mark pushed into Todd's butt as far and as hard as possible, and with his head laying on the mattress right beside Todd's head, he said, "Oh man, oh man! Here it comes man, here it comes! Oh man, I can't believe I'm unloading another load of cum this fast! I have not shot this much cum so fast, in years! Oh, I love having sex with you. You like it so fucking rough and wild, and man, so do I! You are going to let me keep fucking you right? Right? I mean, today's not our only time, right?"

"Hell no it is not the only time! Oh my God no! This is heaven for me man! This is heaven! I think I'm the one that needs to be afraid this won't happen again! Yeah, I'll let you use my ass anytime you want. And remember, you told me a little bit ago, that you'd take me with you when you go to fuck around with some of the other cops, right?"

"Hey man. Let's both quit worrying. I kind of think maybe you're as excited about doing this stuff with me, as I am about using you and that rough, tight, little ass of yours! And yeah – yeah, I'll take you when I go see one of the other guys! Fact is, be kind of fun for me to kind of show you off to them and let them see what I found, and also what I have available for me to use all of the time."

"Oh good! Thank goodness! Yeah, I like being with you, letting you use me, fuck the hell out of me, and it sounds real exciting, the idea of getting to go with you to see some of your other buddies. Oh man, just thinking about doing that kind of makes me feel like if we do that – then I'd kind of be something like the toy boy, to be used and shown off, right? You'd let them fuck me too, right? I'd kind of be the toy for them to use, right? You'd tell them to fuck me, right?"

"Yeah right! I didn't want to put it that way for fear that might be kind of a turn off to you, but since I guess looking at it that way is kind of exciting to you, yeah, I'd take you as the toy for the night! That be OK? Like that?"

"Oh shit yeah! Yeah, I like that idea. Got to admit, I never thought of doing something like that, but man, what an exciting thought! Yeah, the toy for some state cops to play around with and fuck my ass. Oh Mark! God man! Oh yeah, I wanta do that! Yeah I do! How soon can we do that?"

"Well, I don't know right now, but I'll get something set up and get a couple of guys lined up and tell 'em I've got someone that needs some good rough, real rough, ass action! Hey, any problem if one of the guys is a big, very, very, well hung black cop? A guy that hangs about eleven inches or more, and about the size of a coke can around? Want him to fuck you?"

"Oh man, you got a friend like that? A guy that can fuck me? Hell yes I'd want him to fuck me! Why in the hell would I have a problem with that? Oh fuck man that sounds exciting! Shit that sounds exciting, but I've never been fucked by a black man, and I've read and heard they can really fuck the hell out of a guy with the big dicks they have! Oh yeah, do that, please! Yeah, get that set up – please!"

"OK – but as excited as you are with me just mentioning this, maybe I shouldn't do that. If helping you get fucked by too big of a pecker back here, you might not want mine in you anymore!"

"Oh, no chance of that! No chance! The way you fuck! Hey regardless of whatever else I get stuck up in there, or how big some other guy's rod is, I'll always want you and yours! Believe me man, believe me! The way you fuck me is the way I like it. Yeah I really do! Hey, wait, what time is it? How late is it? I need to call the company and have somebody come get me yet. I sent the truck on with Joe and told him, I'd call for somebody to come get me when I was done. Sure did not know how fucking exciting my afternoon was gonna turn out to be, though! Wow, what a great day!"

"Another idea! What do you need to do yet tonight? What if you just called the company, and told 'em you've got a ride, and you'll get your car later. Then we'll have some supper, and then oh – maybe – just maybe – get some grease out and see if that ass of yours is really ready for a fist or not! What do you say? Interested?"

"Oh my God yes I am! Oh, seriously? You seriously mean it? You want me to stay, and then let you see if I can get your fist up in me? Is that what you're saying? Is that right?"

"Think that's what I said! Yeah, think that's what I was kind of suggesting! Want to? Wanna see if this cop guy can get his fist up inside of that ass of yours?"

"Oh hell yes man, oh yes! Oh, I can't really believe you are asking me to stay and do that! Oh, hell yes! Let me call the store and tell them I'll get my car later. Oh – this is gonna be great!"

Todd called the store and told them that he had a ride, not to worry about him getting his car, and after the call, Mark suggested that perhaps they run through the shower and kind of freshen up a little from all of the previous sex actions, and then move to the kitchen for a quick sandwich and a beer. Soon as they had eaten their sandwich and finished the beer, Mark then suggested that they head back to the bedroom.

"Hey Todd, you want some more fucking before we start the hand up in there, or just wanna get going on the hand thing?"

"Oh man, fuck me – fuck me – fuck me! Shit man, I gotta be fucked again first! Oh, the way you fuck me, I gotta have it again!"

Without fanfare, Todd hit the bed, arms out, legs spread and his ass up in the air just waiting for Mark to do his slamming and banging into his ass. Mark, grabbed a little grease, smeared it on his dick and went in without even mentioning that he was ready. Once again, Todd got it rough and tough for about ten minutes.

"I'm gonna get this ass good and open and anxious so we can see just how much of my fist you can get up in there!" Mark told Todd as he repeatedly pounded Todd's already hungry and anxious ass. Once again Mark's body went stiff and rigid as he again grabbed Todd by the chest and pushed his dick up into Todd's ass as far and as hard as he could! "Oh shit man, oh shit! Oh Todd here it comes man, here it comes!"

Once Mark had managed to regain some of his strength after, once again, another hot climax into Todd's ass, he reached over to the night stand, took the dish of Crisco that he had brought into the bedroom after the sandwich, and he told Todd. "Oh man, this is it! All I want you to do is lay there, trust me, let me do my thing back here, and just relax your ass. OK? Can you do that?"

"Oh God I hope so! Oh, I want you to do this so much, but oh man, I am so fucking scared right now I don't know how to just lay here! Hey, if it hurts too much, can I ask you to stop? Oh my God man! Only a few days ago I had never even been with a man, and now, all of a sudden, I'm gonna let you try an put your fist up in my ass? Oh man am I fucking crazy or something? Oh man, I'm scared, I really am!"

Letting Todd express his fears and concerns, Mark decided, was definitely good for Todd. Mark knew that if he tried to shut him up, that would only frustrate Todd that much more, and beside, he felt that the more he let him talk, that was using up some of the bent up nervous energy that he simply knew Todd was filled with right now. Mark remembered the first time he had taken a man's hand up in his ass, and he remembered well how fucking scared and nervous he was. Out in an old barn, following a wild late night party of some 15 or 20 gay guys, and he knew that if he did not do it that night, he was never gonna hear the end of it from his buddies. Five guys had all taken a fist for their first time that night, and he was next, as far as his buddies were concerned! No, 'yes or no', more of a, 'get your ass up on the table and let ole Jake get at it! Scared and nervous as hell, but having to stand his honor, Mark did it! Now, it was Todd's turn to be scared and nervous!

Todd spread eagle out on the bed, and Mark could hear him repeatedly keep taking big deep breaths. Mark said nothing. He felt that right now it was more important for some good silent time, and to let Todd attempt to get calm, and at the same time, allow Todd the fun and excitement, as frightening as it might be, realizing that he truly was just about to get a man's fist, pushed up into his ass. Not a dick, not a dildo, not a broom handle – a fist! A man's whole hand!

Getting everything neatly arranged so that everything he might want or need, was handy, Mark put on a pair of surgical gloves, and he then spread a rather good amount of Crisco onto, and into, Todd's ass. Even this action made Todd jerk and move. Even this little amount of ass action felt good and made him push his ass up in the air some, as if to say, "Here it is, come and get it!" Slowly Mark worked the Crisco into Todd's ass by slightly pulling on the edges of the hole, and sliding first one finger, then two fingers in, both pushing Crisco as they went.

"Oh man! Oh man, yeah, that feels good! Oh, yeah I can feel your fingers up in there! Yeah – yeah! Oh, I can feel 'em! Oh, I like that! Oh that feels so good!"

"Good! I'm glad that feels good! That'll help get this tight ass of yours all good and open. You lay there and enjoy this, OK? Your ass will feel real good, real good!"

Slowly Mark used one finger to do some deep protruding, and then he added another. Once again slowly he massaged the interior of Todd's butt, and once again he heard Todd exclaim how great that felt up in there.

As Mark continued to service Todd's asshole, inside and out, he encouraged, "Hang on man, it's gonna get better!"

Without Todd even realizing it, Mark added a third finger. He was now using three fingers up, and in, as far as possible, and also an additional finger from his left hand to encourage Todd's butt hole to slightly open just a little more. Slowly and gently Mark continued to work on the hole, and occasionally he would encourage Todd to "Just lay there and relax. Everything's OK back here! Still anxious to feel that hand up in there?"

"Oh yes, oh yes! Oh God I think so, I think so! But I'm still scared, I really am!"

"Being scared is part of the fun! Just relax and let me do my thing! Everything's gonna be OK!"

Slowly and carefully Mark continued his quest of gaining total access to Todd's insides. Slowly he worked Todd's ass, now with all four fingers, and slowly he pushed and twisted to gain additional depth. Todd was accepting this very easily for a first timer. He was letting his fister know that he was truly enjoying this, even though he still admitted to being scared.

Using all four fingers on his right hand, in addition to some additional help from the other hand, Mark slid his thumb in place so that it was now a process of just getting that hole open far enough to let his whole hand slide in. He knew the process would be very time consuming, and he had let Todd know that if they were successful in accomplishing this, it was not going to happen 'all of a sudden'. Todd was well aware that if getting a fist up in him was possible, it was going to take a very experienced top, some time, some patience, some anxiety, some desire, and an asshole opened farther then it had ever been opened before! All elements were necessary if they were to be successful. And at this point in time, it did look like everything was perfectly in place, except for maybe the wide open asshole. That part of the equation. Mark was definitely working on.

"Todd, you're doing good man, doing good! How you feeling? Everything OK?"

"Oh yeah, it's OK. My ass feels really full and really spread open, but man, I still want to know that I took your fist, so please, keep pushing! I can feel every time you move your hand and when you push on me stronger. Every time you push, I wonder if it's gonna just go on in me! Can it do that? When you push, will it just go in?"

"Well, that's pretty hard to answer. Yeah, I gotta push to make it go in, but I don't want to let you think that it will just automatically fall in. You're gonna know it pretty well when it's about to go in. Todd, your ass is gonna feel real pressure when my knuckles get right there. Then when my knuckles snap in, you will definitely know you have my fist up in there. Now when my hand goes up and in, it is gonna hurt for a moment. That's just cause we managed to spread that muscle just enough, for a moment to let my knuckles slide in, so when that happens, just lay there and be calm. Todd, don't try to shit my hand back out! Let it stay there and let your ass close around my wrist. Seriously man, it will quit hurting in just a moment. As soon as you realize you have taken that hand, you are gonna have a smile on your face. Then you'll probably beg for me to put it in deeper and deeper."

"Oh I don't know! Man, right now I just know that if I can get it up in there, I'll be glad. The deeper and deeper stuff, I don't think so! Right now I just want to get your hand up in there so I can know we did it! How we doing? Are we gonna do it?"

"We are doing good! Real good! You do have one hungry asshole back here man! They are right! Your ass is hungry and ready for some wild assed action! You just keep laying there and let me do my thing back here! We're making progress, we just need to take it good and slow!"

As if these two men had known each other for years, and had planned this session for a long time, Todd continued to offer his bare ass to Mark's hand, and continued to beg for more, more, and more. Todd wanted to know that he had been successful on his first attempt of getting a man's hand put up in, his ass. Mark's hand – the big man's hand!

Mark continued to work on this, 'hand virgin ass,' and continued to be amazed at how fast Todd was taking the spreading and the pressure, of the true fact, that he was actually getting fisted! He pushed, turned and actually just played with Todd's ass as he continued to watch more and more of his hand slide into Todd's butt.

"Ouch, ouch! Oh Mark, what's happening? That hurt's now! Wow, what going on?"

"What is going on is you are just about to take a fist up in your ass. Lay still there and try to relax. This is where I told you about my knuckles. Well, we're there! I can not believe how fucking fast we have gotten to this point. Are you sure you never had a fist up in here before?"

"No, no! No, the only thing I've had up in there is a couple of dicks and those dildos that Dave used on me! That's all, seriously man, that's all."

"Well, let me tell you man, as fast as we gotten this little butt hole to open up for my hand, I guess right now I'd like to see just how big of a dildo did that guy use on you! Hell – right now, I'm kinda surprised he didn't just fist you that night!"

"Oh, ohhhh! Oh man – oh man!! Oh shit man, I can feel your hand! Oh man it is really pressing on my ass! Oh Mark, oh Mark – is it gonna go in? Is it gonna go in?"

"Lay still. Let me grab you and hug you! Lay there, I'm getting close! Real close! It's taken us some time here man, but I'm getting close! I can't believe that you are actually gonna take a hand your very first time trying. Hang on man, hang on, it's about to slide in! I can tell – it's just about to go in! Oh – here it goes – hang on man – hang on!"

"Ouch, oh shit! Ouch! Damn man that hurts! Oh God that hurts! Oh my ass, oh my ass! Oh shit, that hurts!"

"Lay still, lay still, lay still! Don't move! Just lay there! My hand went in! Lay there! Relax! Don't try to push it out! Just lay there!"

"Oh my God! Oh shit! Oh God Mark! I've got your hand up in me, don't I? Your hand's up in me, isn't it?"

"Yeah. Yeah, it sure is! You doing OK? Just lay there! I'm gonna hold my hand real steady for a minute to let you relax on it! You OK?"

"How in the hell can somebody be OK that just did that? Oh man! Yeah, I'm OK but shit man, now I think I know what a woman feels when she pops a kid out! Oh yeah, I'm OK. Oh, I can feel all of your hand up in there now. Yeah, it quit hurting, but man, I was afraid you tore my ass open. Wow! Whoa, what a feeling! Yeah – we did it and I like it! Hey, can you move your fingers around in there so I can feel them? Oh man, that is great! Oh shit yeah, keep that up! I like that! Oh yeah, yeah. Oh man, feels like I got me some kind of a little critter up in my ass when you move your fingers! Oh Mark, that feels good! Really different than anything I've ever felt before, but man, I like it! Oh Mark – I've been fisted! Wow! I can't believe this! You like feeling my insides? This good for you? You glad we did this!?"

"Hell yeah I'm glad! Shit man. I knew your ass was gonna feel good on my hand, and I sure as hell was right! You got a state trooper up inside of you man, a state trooper! Bet you never thought the first guy to stick his hand up inside of your ass, was gonna be a state trooper, did you?"

"Oh hell no! Oh, I've seen so many pictures of cops with their night stick held up against some guy's ass, I would have figured if I got it from a cop, it's probably be his night stick he rammed up in my ass! Oh shit man, wait till I tell David I got fisted by one of our state's finest. Hell, even without being a cop, to me, you are still one of the state's finest! I wish I could step back and just see you laying here on me, with you hand stuck up in my ass! Oh man, what a picture that would be!"

"How's your ass feeling? Feeling OK?"

"Yeah man, it's OK! Feeling full as hell, but feeling good that way! I am weird, ain't I? Shit man, it's only been like two weeks since I got my first fucking, and now I'm into getting fisted. Guys don't usually move that fast do they?"

"You know Todd, maybe some do! You're not 18 anymore, and I guess you and your body were just real ready for this type of action, and it just took you a little while to finally find it and get it going for you! I don't know, maybe internally you are making up for lost time!"

"Oh shit man, I will say one thing – internally right now, my internals are feeling really full, and I feel like I'm making up for a hell of a lot of lost time. Oh yeah man, I wish I had done this years ago. I wish I had started this when I was still 18. Mark, does a guy's ass get used to getting a fist up in it, so that it will kind of automatically open up right away for it. Does it get easier each time you get fisted?"

"No. No, your ass will slam shut once I pull out of it! Sure each time you do it you're that much more anxious for it. Tonight you weren't sure of what was gonna happen, so you were scared. Next time you'll know what to expect, and you're just gonna be anxious to get that hand up in you, as quick as you can, so you can feel what you are feeling, right now. Understand?"

"Yeah, I guess. Yeah, I think I do. Oh yeah, move your hand around in there! Let me feel your hand pushing on my insides. Oh man, that feels so good!"

Mark continued to fist, and play in Todd's ass for probably 15 or maybe 20 minutes more when they decided that maybe enough for one night was enough.

"OK man, lay still! I'm gonna pull it back out and yeah, you are gonna feel it, but not like when it went in you. Lay still and relax! Here goes! Lay still!"

"Ouch, oh shit man! Ouch! Oh, shit man! Damn I could feel your knuckles pop back out! Oh man, what a feeling! Yeah, I felt it when your hand opened me back up to come back out, but it didn't hurt like when it went in. Yeah, I can tell my ass slammed shut. Oh man, feels like it should be standing wide open! Wow! Oh man, thank you for doing that! Really man, thank you a lot! I can't believe I got a fist up in my ass, and shit man, I got it by one of the hottest looking cops in the state! Hell man – probably the hottest cop in the state! Wow! What a trip! Thanks man – thank you!"

"Hey, it's not all me! If you weren't one of the hottest looking guys running around town, there's no way I would have even suggested this! You are a pretty hot stud on your own!"

"Well, thanks for that! Now, all I need to do is go find that other guy, that you thought I was earlier today, and tell him how damn glad I look like him. It sure paid off for me today! But believe me, if I ever find him, I sure as hell am not gonna tell him what he missed. I'm too fucking greedy! I'm not gonna share you, if I can help it!"

CHAPTER NINE:

Too Hunky of a Guy, To Leave Behind

"Hello, this it Todd." Todd's phone rang, and he had no idea of who in the world would be calling him at this time of night.

"Hello, Todd Underwood?"

"Yeah, yes it is, who's calling?"

"Todd this is James Wilson. You installed some carpeting in our house a couple of weeks ago, right? You know Gary Wilson, right? Gary, he's my boy."

"Yeah, yes I did, and yes I know Gary. Yeah, OK. So – it's like almost midnight – what do you want?"

The mention of Gary's name made Todd just a little nervous, when he heard Mr. Wilson mention it, and he immediately decided he needed to see just why Gary's father was calling him – at that time of night.

"Uh, Todd, everything is OK! Understand? Please understand everything is OK! I know you and Gary have become – what should I say – some pretty close friends, right?"

Now being very, very concerned, since he and Gary had made it together again, after their first session, Todd was getting a little more than just a little uncomfortable, that Mr. Wilson was on the phone –

this time of night, and was now mentioning that he knew that Gary and he had become "pretty close friends," as he called it.

"Yeah, we know each other. He OK? Something wrong?"

"No Todd, no! Everything is OK! Uh – Todd, I know you and Gary have been making it with each other lately. It's OK – listen Todd – it's OK! I'm not calling you to scare you. What you two do together is OK. Please understand me, it's OK!"

"OK, so why are you calling me then? What in the hell is going on?"

"Todd, be patient with me a minute. This is pretty hard for me right now. Uh – you home by yourself? You by yourself?

"Yeah, yeah I am, but so what? Mr. Wilson, why are you calling me?"

"First, please don't call me Mr. Wilson. Please just call me Jim. Todd, I want to come over. Can I come over? I'd like to talk to you."

"Come over? Why in the hell do you want to come over? What are you talking about?"

"Oh, I'm so sorry, I'm really having trouble here. Oh, I don't know how to say this. Uh Todd – uh Todd, I want to play with you like Gary does. Oh man, I want to have sex with you like Gary did!"

"What!? What did you say!?" Todd almost screamed back into the phone.

"Wait, please be patient with me. I'm trying to tell what I want, but I've got to admit, I'm shaking in my shoes just making this call. Todd, I saw you guys in Gary's bedroom the other day. I watched and I wanted to come in and be part of what you guys were doing. Gary thought I was gone for the day when he had you come over, but I had to come home to get some papers that I forgot, and that's when I saw what was happening. Todd, please, can you and I do some stuff?"

"Oh shit man! So you just stood there and watched us have sex? Is that what you are saying? Is that right?"

"Yeah, yes I did. I'm not proud of it, but it looked so fucking good to me, it got me so fucking turned on, I couldn't just turn around and walk away! I watched both of you guys suck on each other, and

I watched you fuck Gary's ass, and then he got up on top of you, and he fucked yours. You kept yelling for more, more!"

"Oh shit man, I can't believe this! So did you tell Gary that you watched us?"

"Oh no! Oh no! No, I can't do that! I can't let Gary know I called you either! Please, please don't tell him about this call, please! I can't let him know anything about you and I talking. Please!"

"Yeah OK, I hear you, but I'm still confused. Why did you call. Why did you say you wanted to come over here? Did you ask if we could do some stuff? Did you actually say you wanted to have sex with me like I did with Gary? Is that what you said? Is that what you said? Is that right?

"Yeah, yeah that's what I said. Todd, I would love to be in bed with you. I really want to have sex with you. I really do! I kind of did that once – one time, when I was a freshman in college, and I've never done it since then, and after watching you two, I really want to do it again, and you are the only guy I know to ask. I don't know any other gay guys to call! Oh watching you guys doing that together made me have such a fucking big hardon. I was standing there wanting to pull it out and jerk it off so bad! Oh it made me hard and stiff. I didn't know until then how much I've been wanting to make it with a guy. Oh, please, can we? Please, oh Todd, please!"

"How in the hell did you even get my phone number to call me? If you haven't told Gary you watched, how did you get my number.

"Oh, I looked at Gary's cell phone this afternoon when he left it on the table. I knew your first name was Todd, so I looked and found it. Please don't be mad that I did. I know I should not have looked, but I sure couldn't ask him what your number was! We can't let him know about this! Please, can I come over? Just for a little time. I really want to do it. Ever since I stood there and watched you guys, I've just been out of my mind wanting to do this. I told my wife I had to be gone overnight, just so I could be out of the house for a while. I'm supposed to be out of town on business today. Please, may I come over to your place, or you come over here to the motel, please?"

"Wow, man oh man! I never expected to ever get this type of a phone call. Yeah, I guess. Mr. Wilson, I mean, Jim, you sure about this? Really you are not pissed that you caught Gary and I doing it? Seriously, I'm not in some big fucking trouble if I let you come over here?"

"No Todd, you sure are not in trouble. Even if you say we can't do anything, I still won't be mad. Gary's a grown kid. He's old enough to do whatever he wants, and it's not up to me to be his policeman. No, no – I'm not mad. I'm just fucking anxious to get another chance to do this with a guy, and you looked pretty damn hot when you were with Gary. I know I'm begging now, but please I haven't thought about doing anything else since I watched you two making it together. Todd, I've even jerked off twice each day since then, and I will admit, it's been years and years since I've jerked off. Oh man, I am so fucking hot for this, can we please?"

"Shit man, I'm getting really kind of confused here! Gary and I are doing some stuff together, you watched us, and now you want to do it with me? Is that right?"

"Yeah Todd, yeah that's right! Please? If you don't want me coming to your place, you can come here. I'm at the Country Hill Motel on Rt. 54. Please, please! You have no idea how much nerve it took to just make this call to you. Really man, I drove around for probably two hours just hoping to find some guy out on the street that I could bring back here, just so I didn't have to call you and tell you what I want. I couldn't find anybody. I finally decided that if I was gonna have to call you, I'd better do it before it got any later. Oh Todd – can we?"

"I guess, I guess. Got to admit, this is way too weird, but if you are that fucking hungry for it, I guess so. What room are you in? I'll come over there. It'll take me about 30 minutes to get there though. You sure about this? You're not gonna change your mind once I get there, are you?"

"Oh no Todd, no I sure won't. Oh thanks man, thanks! Oh hurry man, hurry! I'm anxious for this! Oh Todd, you have no idea of what this means to me!"

"Well, let me tell you, I don't think it could be any more weird or feel any more funny on your end for you than it is over here for me! I mean after all! I fuck some nice young guy, and a few days later his dad calls, tells me he watched us go at it, he hasn't done this except for once back in college, and now he wants me to fuck around with him too? I hope like hell I'm not getting set up for a beating or something. I never thought I'd have some guy's father call, and then tell me he wants to fuck around too, and especially after he watched me fuck his own son. I may be stupid as hell, but yeah, I'll come over there! Hope like hell I don't regret this later though!"

Todd got the room number and actually wrote a note – of where he was headed, and who he was supposed to meet, and left it on the kitchen table, so that just in case he did not return, somebody would find it. He liked the idea of doing it with Gary's dad, even though he had no idea of what the man even looked like, but yet he was still nervous about this mysterious type of a meeting. The unknowing of just what Mr. Wilson was like, was part of Todd's suspense and excitement! He was actually going out, in the middle of the night to have sex, gay sex, and with some guy he had no idea of just what he was like. But he could not escape the knowing, that this is Gary's dad. The idea that he would now have played around with, and fucked, both Gary and his dad, was a real turn on. For somebody that just started doing the guy thing, so recently, Todd knew he was getting to do some sessions, and some playing around, that a lot of much more experienced guys had never done. He wondered just how many guys have had the chance to fuck a guy, and then have that guy's father actually call and tell him he wants to fuck around too.

For Mr. Wilson to call and be pissed off about him having sex with his son – that he could understand, but for him to call and actually be glad it was happening, and that he wants to be part of the action, now that was pretty hard for Todd to accept.

Getting to the County Hill Motel and finding that room number 86 was well in the back area of the motel, Todd decided that Jim Wilson certainly did not want anybody to just happen to see him going into a motel room. Todd knocked on the door. Quickly, very quickly, the door opened and Todd realized that the man, opening the door, was fully naked! He pulled the door open, and made no attempt of hiding his full nudity, nor even his full hardon. Stunned and shocked, Todd took a gasp, and after checking out the eight and a half inch rod that was pointing at himself, he asked, "Jim Wilson? Are you Jim?"

"Oh yeah Todd, yeah! Come on in man, come on in! Oh Todd, thanks for coming! Thanks!"

"Shit man, shit! Damn man, I sure did not expect to be greeted quite this way! Hi, I'm Todd Underwood."

Extending his hand out to shake hands with Todd, Jim replied, "Oh man, I am so damn glad you agreed to come. I know this is weird, but man, I just had to see if we could get together and do some stuff together. I'm sorry I'm acting so goofy, but man, like I said, after I saw you and Gary having sex together, I have not been able to think of anything else! Watching you guys doing that was hot, fucking hot man! I've never watched two guys fucking each other, or even sucking on each other, and man that really turned me on! Man, I'm so glad you're here!"

Looking around slightly, Todd finally asked, Uh – Jim. We here by ourselves? Just you and me?"

"Yeah, yeah – just you and me. Why? Think somebody else would be here?"

"No! Just being a little uncomfortable with a guy's dad calling me, in the middle of the night, telling me he watched me fuck his son, and now he wants to do the same thing. Not exactly what somebody would expect. I just want to be sure this is not a set up, to really get at me, for fucking around with Gary."

"No, it's no set up Todd! No! Seriously man, I just want you and I do some playing around. Nothing funny man – nothing funny is going on. I'm just begging that you'll let me do some stuff with you! After watching you two go at it, I really, really, want to do what I watched you guys do! I've never done it with a guy and now I want to, and I want to do it tonight! Oh please, I want us to have sex, OK?"

Looking around and finally deciding that they were all by themselves, Todd slowly started to calm himself down and accept what Jim was telling him. "You want you and me to have sex, right? You don't intend to beat the hell out of me for having sex with your boy, right? I mean, let's face it! The way you are built, you could beat me to a pulp in a second. Seriously man, you are strong and you could kill me if you wanted just by strangling me or something. That's why I decided to come over here, instead of letting you come to my place. I figured if you're gonna do anything to me, better be here where somebody will find me. I'm safe, right? Really, the fact I fucked Gary is OK with you? You just want me and you to have some sex, right?"

"Yeah, right – right! That's all, that's all. But please, we can't let Gary know about this. Seriously man, I can't let anybody know about this. I can't let anybody know I played around with a guy! I'm serious! I'm fucking horny to play with you, and I'm damn anxious to do this, but I can't let anybody find out about this! This has got to be our secret, OK?"

"Yeah, I guess so, I guess so! Got to admit though, this is really weird! Fuck some guy and then have his dad call and say he wants the same thing! I'm game, I mean shit man, look at you! You are one hot looking dude! Maybe we met in a real funny way, but I will admit that if we had met in a bar or someplace, I'd have been all over you trying to get in your pants. You are one hot stud! If I'd have met you someplace else, everything would be kind of normal, but just knowing you are Gary's Dad, wow, that makes this feel kind of funny. You sure you're Gary's Dad? You sure you're not just one of his older brothers? To know, that I fucked a boy and then fucked his dad too, wow, that feels kind of weird!"

As Jim reached down and grabbed his own hardon and shook it in front of Todd, he pleaded, "Please, please grab this! Let me feel you grab my dick! I really wanna feel your hand on my dick!"

Todd looked down, watched Jim jerk his rod back and forth a few times and watched him actually make it harder than it was before, and he then took a total look at Jim, head to toe.

"You are Gary's dad, right? This is not some fake thing – you really are Gary's dad?"

"Yeah, I am, yeah. I'm Gary's dad. You don't believe me?"

"Well, I don't know! Gary's like what, 21, right? How old were you when you had Gary? Shit man, you don't look old enough to be his father. How old are you anyway?"

I'm 49. I was 20 years old when we had Bobby, Gary's older brother."

"Shit man, for being 49 you sure as hell are in good shape! You a coach or something?"

"No, I'm a company president. Company that sells vitamins and supplements and stuff like that, so yeah, I need to keep myself in pretty good shape. Gotta look like I use the stuff we sell."

"Well, shit man, you sure as hell do! I mean you do look like you use something. And I can sure as hell see just where Gary gets that big dick of his! He's hung just like you! Shit man, now I'm wishing I could see what his older brothers are hung like! I'll bet they're hung just like you two guys are! Right? A good part of the family genes, I guess! I mean, Gary's hung like a horse, and now I see he's hung like his dad! Guess maybe his brothers have to be hung pretty good too, right?"

"Really, is Gary pretty well hung? I mean, I haven't seen his dick for so long, I've kind of wondered for a long time now of how well he's hung. That day you and he were together was the closest for me to get a chance to see it, but I never got a good view of it. When he got up on you, he poked your ass so fast, I never got to really see it. So it's pretty good sized, right?"

"Oh yeah, right! Big, and feels like a glory pole up in my ole asshole! Feels good!"

"Hey man, you gonna get undressed? I'm standing here all naked and supporting this raging hardon, and you're still dressed. You gonna get your clothes off?"

"Yeah, yeah I am! I mean, looking at you all naked there, and especially with that fucking enormous stiff pole on you, you better be sure I'm gonna get naked! I'm getting real anxious for you and I, to do some stuff together, now. Jim, I'm getting real glad you got up the nerve to call me. Yeah, I wanna fuck you. I wanna feel my dick going up in those tight butt muscles. Yeah, I want to see if you can feel my dick up in there! You want fucked?"

As Todd quickly started to remove his clothes, he looked up at Jim to see if he was going to get an answer for his question.

"Well, – I asked man – I asked. You want to get fucked?"

"Oh – oh shit man! Yeah, I guess! Oh man, I never even thought about the possibility of me getting fucked. For some reason in my excitement, I guess all I thought about was you and I just being together and feeling each other, and definitely me fucking that ass of yours. I watched it a lot when you were fucking Gary's butt, and Todd, you have got one hot ass. I mean it man, it is hot! I guess I never really thought about any other details of what we'd be doing once we were together. Seriously man, I never thought about me getting it up in the ass. All I thought about was how I really wanted to poke yours. Shit man, I never thought about me getting fucked. Guess I was only thinking one sided. Hey you know us married guys. We only think about doing the fucking, never about getting fucked! But Todd, I do know I really do want a chance at that ass of yours! Man, I've dreamt about getting in it ever since that day I watched you and Gary together. Your ass is so pretty!"

"Hey man, you want some sex, and there ain't nothing better than getting a dick up in your ass! I know for damn sure – you are gonna fuck me with that damn rod of yours before I leave here! I know that for damn sure! I sure as hell am not gonna be in a bedroom with a dick like that and not have it up in my ass!"

Todd finished getting himself all undressed, and he then stood up in front of Jim and let him see his hardon. "Come on man, grab it! Let me feel you grab it!"

Looking directly at Todd with a big smile on his face, Jim reached out and solidly took a hold of Todd's dick.

"Yeah man, yeah! That feels good, pull it! Yeah pull on it!"

"Oh, I can't believe this! I can't believe this! Seriously man, ever since I watched you and Gary going at it, I've been praying for this. I did this just once in my life, and all of a sudden, I just had to do it again. Can we kind of suck on each other? I've never done that before, and I want to so bad now. I want to see what it's like."

"So that time in college, you didn't suck on that guy? What'd you guys do?"

"Oh man! At that time I thought we did so much, but now I'm not so sure we really did much of anything. I guess we were both too scared. He did suck on me for a minute, but I never sucked on him.

I jerked him off and felt his ass, and he ran a finger up in my ass, but then I made him pull it back out. We were in the locker room of the gym and I guess we were so damn afraid somebody would come in, that's all we did. So, can I do it now? Can we suck on each other? I want to finally see what having a dick in my mouth is like. OK?"

"Yeah sure we can, of course! Not so sure I can get all of that rod of yours in my mouth, but I can try. Guess I'll just have to remember how I did it when I took Gary's. Gagged like hell, but I finally managed. Now I get to do his Daddy's. Hey, this is kind of exciting!"

Todd and Jim laid down on the bed and immediately went into the ole usable 69 position and took the other man's rod into his hands. Todd immediately took Jim's rod into his mouth and tried to swallow as much of it as he could. Jim stroked Todd's dick and took a minute or two to actually start putting his mouth on it. Slowly, but firmly, he started taking it, and Todd knew that sucking on a guy's dick for the first time, was a pretty nervous thing for Jim to be doing. Pulling off of Jim's rod, Todd softly encouraged Jim with, "Yeah man! Yeah! Oh man that feels good! Glad you're doing that? Yeah, keep it up, keep it up – that feels good! Yeah man, yeah take all of it! Take it man, take it!"

Jim slowly managed to take all of Todd's rod, and rather quickly he appeared to be a quick learning, true, cock sucker. He was using Todd as if he was a true professional. Man to man, face to crotch, cock to mouth and beyond, the two men were involved in each other like they had been partners for years. Todd was using Jim's enormous rod to his fullest enjoyment, and to him it was obvious that even though this might be Jim's first time sucking on another man's cock, he was truly into it and truly enjoying it.

As they laid there enjoying each other, and the rods on each other, Todd suggested, "Hey big man. My ass is really anxious to feel you up in there! Ready to fuck my butt man with this big rod? You ready?"

Jim immediately pulled off of Todd and quickly answered, "Oh God yes man, oh yes! Oh Todd ever since I watched that ass of yours pump up and down when you were fucking Gary, I've wanted to feel me pushing in on you, yeah man, yeah, let me fuck your ass!"

Not knowing if Jim would be prepared, or even know, that he needed to be prepared, Todd pulled a small tube of KY out of his pants pocket and coated Jim's rod and also slid a little up into his own ass.

"There man, I'm ready! I'm gonna lay down and you lay on top of me. Got to admit, even though you may not be aware of it, I'm pretty new to this too, so when you start in, go kind of slow until I get opened up enough to take all of you, OK?"

"Oh yeah, yeah, I will! Oh man I've wanted to do this pretty ass for days and days now. Oh, Todd I can't believe I am actually getting to lay on top of you and play with you. Oh, I wanna lick and suck on you some, before I push my dick up in there, OK?"

"Yeah man, yeah! Hey, I'm here for you to use and enjoy. I'm trying to make this session as fun for you as possible. Jim, I've got to tell you, I sure don't want this to be our only session. You are so fucking hot! Really man, you look like you should be one of Gary's older brothers, not his dad! I hope like hell I can look as hot as you do when I'm your age! I love feeling and touching you, and of course, you damn well know, you've got the dick of death on you. Kiss my ass, lick my butt! Hey, if that KY I put up in my ass is in the way, wipe it out so you can bite my ass if you want. I do know I love to have somebody pull my butt apart and get his face right up at my asshole and bite the edge of it!"

"Oh shit, really? Really, can I do that? Can I actually bite on the edge of your asshole? Can I!?"

"Hell yes man, hell yes! You bite my ass and when I get on top of you, I'll bite yours and let you see just how fucking hot it is! Yeah man, do it! Bite me!"

Jim took the instructions and without hesitation. He had his face firmly planted right up against Todd's asshole and managed to get the edge of Todd's butt hole in his mouth – and he bit."

"Oh yeah man – oh yes! Yeah bite it, bite it! Oh yeah that feels so fucking damn good'! Oh I love that! Oh God I am so glad you finally got the nerve to call me tonight. Scared the hell out of me at first, since I figured you probably wanted to beat the hell out of me for fucking around with your boy, but man, this is working out great. Yeah, bite me, yeah – bite harder!"

Todd continued to push his ass up in the air so that Jim could push his face in good and solid, and he kept begging for Jim to bite and to bite harder. Finally Jim could not resist any longer.

"Oh Todd, I've got to fuck you, I've got to fuck you!"

Immediately the two men rearranged themselves, and Jim found the eager and anxious hole that Todd was making available to him.

"Oh go slow – go slow man – go slow! Oh shit Jim, your dick is so fucking big going in back there! Yeah man push, but push slow! Let me get my ass opened up for it. Yeah, push, just go kind of slow. How you doing, how's it going?"

"Oh man it's going good! Oh, I can not believe I have actually got my dick up in this pretty little tight ass of yours! Oh what a feeling! You OK? You taking this OK?"

"Yeah man, yeah! Yeah I'm doing OK! Keep pushing, keep pushing! Oh man, it feels like I've got your boy Gary up in me again! Oh man you guys have got big cocks! Oh Jim I feel like I'm getting all of it – ain't I? You got about all of your dick up in me?"

"Yeah, I do! Yeah, oh yeah, there, that's it man! I'm all up in you! Oh yeah, I'm pushing on your ass! Yeah, you've got it man, you've got it! You OK?"

"Oh shit yes man, hell yes! Oh man that big rod of yours, up in there, feels so fucking good! Push on me man, push on my ass!"

"I am, I am! Can I kind of pull out some and then push it back in? Can I do that?"

"Oh hell yes you can, yes you can! I'm open for it now! My ass is real ready to really get fucked now! Jim, fuck the hell out of it now! Slam my ass, fuck me hard! Use me and use my ass! Fuck me hard! You can fuck harder this time than anytime you've ever fucked before. Fuck me hard man! Fuck me hard! Oh use my ass!"

Immediately and without further instructions, Jim did! He started fucking Todd's ass like it was some concrete sidewalk being broken up!

"Oh shit man, is this too rough? Is this hurting?"

"No, it's not too hard and hell no, it's not hurting! Keep it up! Oh Jim that big rod of yours is so fucking good up in there, yeah man, yeah! Keep it up, keep it up!"

"Oh, oh – Todd, I'm about to cum!! Oh, I can't hold it! I can't hold it, I gotta cum man, I gotta!"

"Yeah, yeah! Yeah cum man, cum! Let it fly! Shoot me! Let me feel your jazz up in my ass! Oh yeah – oh – yeah, oh it's so fucking warm! Oh my God man – how much you dumping in me? Oh man I can still feel you dumping and shooting in me! Oh my God man, you're still cumming man – you're still cumming! Holy shit man! Jim, I've felt you shoot off in me at least five or six times and each one felt like a cannon going off! God of God man! My ass must be full of your juices man, I must be full! Oh man, you still breathing?"

As Jim totally and completely collapsed fully on top of Todd's prone body, he attempted to answer, but was completely out of breath!

"Oh wait, wait. I need to catch my breath!"

"Hey lay there man, just lay on me for a minute! God man, I know I haven't been with too many guys yet myself, but shit man, I know damn well most guys can't shoot off like that! What in the hell does your wife say when you unload that much in her? What in the hell does she say?"

After regaining his breath somewhat, Jim managed to say, "Todd, I've never – never shot off like that before! Oh Todd, I was wondering if I was ever gonna stop! Really man, I have never shot like that before. Man, my whole body was just going off like firecrackers! Wow – what a fucking feeling! Oh man! Fuck and shit man, I knew I was really anxious to get in that ass of yours after I saw it up in the air so nice and shiny in Gary's bedroom, but man oh man – I never expected something like that! Oh shit man, I'm fucking exhausted! I am exhausted!"

Jim rested on top of Todd, and as he started to roll off to Todd's side, he exclaimed, "Oh shit man! Hey wait! My cum is cumming out of your ass! It's streaming out, like a flowing hose. Hey, let me get something to wipe you up. Shit man, I guess I must have filled that hole of yours. Man, I did not know I even had that much cum in me! Hey, stay there. Let me get some toilet paper."

After Jim tidied Todd's ass area up some, Todd then looked at Jim and asked. "Hey man. I kind of think that after that little cumin session, I might be wrong, but I'm kind of under the impression that fucking your ass tonight is not a real probability, right?"

"Oh shit, I think you're right. As much as I wanna try that, I'm pooped man, I'm pooped. Fucking your ass like that really took it out of me, it did! God man, I have never, even when I was a lot younger, I have never cum like that! I thought I was gonna explode! Oh yeah, I want to, but Todd, I'm beat. I'm fucking beat right now!"

"Hey Jim, don't fret. Like I said earlier, I sure don't want this to be our only session, so let's plan on doing that later, OK?"

"Yeah, OK, but I feel bad since I've dumped my juices and I came, but you haven't. I feel bad about that!"

"Hey, tell you what! Why don't you just lay there and let me straddle you and let me jerk off on your chest! OK? Yeah, got to admit, I'm pretty anxious to let it fly after that fucking I just got, so how bout if I just jerk off on you. That's a pretty good turn on to me anyway. I wanta sit there and watch your face while I let my juice fly all over the front of you! OK? Can I do that?"

"Oh shit man, that sounds like fun! Oh yeah, I'd like that! Let's do that!"

With that encouragement, Todd straddled Jim's body and it only took about a minute for Todd to be letting out the ole hollering, that he was getting ready to cum. "Oh my God, I'm cumin man, I'm cumin! Oh Jim here it comes!"

Suddenly, without further warning, Todd was shooting all of his juices all over Jim's massive chest! Squirt after squirt, Todd sprayed Jim's chest. Jim laid there with his eyes wide open watching the end of Todd's dick shoot out its juices. Three big squirts, and each one got just a little higher on Jim's chest. The last one landed right under his chin and landed on his Adams apple!

"Oh shit man! Oh man! I've never watched another guy shoot off like that! Man I like that! Wow! What a sight to be laying here and watching you shoot all over me! Damn man! Never thought about something like that happening! Shit man, that was hot! Oh Todd, I can't believe that I'm this excited about having some guy sitting on top of me and jerking off his dick onto me! Oh, I never expected to ever feel this way. Shit man, this is outrageous! Fucking outrageous!"

"Oh wow! Shit man, now I'm the one that is exhausted! Damn, that felt good! So you like that, uh? You like watching my jazz come flying out of the end of my rod at you, uh?"

"Oh, I've never seen anything like that before! Yeah, I've watched my own cum flying out of my dick, but that's the first time I've ever been in this position watching some other guy jerk it off and let it fly. It was flying right at my face! Hey man, we've got to do that again sometime, OK?"

"Hey, like I said before, I sure don't want to this to be our only time together, so of course we can. You know Jim. For a guy, well actually maybe even kind of an older guy, one with a bunch of kids, and being a guy that has never played with some other guy before, you sure do learn fast! I'm glad Gary and I are fucking buddies, but I've got to admit, now that I've got to meet his Daddy, this makes it even better. Gary is good, but I kind of think his Daddy is gonna be a whole lot better! I'm glad we did this. And hell, I guess I'm even more glad that you stayed there and watched Gary and I fucking around. I can't imagine what it must be like for a Daddy to be standing there and actually watching his son get fucked in the ass, and then fuck some other guy in the ass – but it sure is paying off for me! Who in the world would ever think that once a guy's dad finds his own son getting fucked in the ass by some other guy, that the Daddy would actually call that guy, and tell him he wants to do that same thing? Seriously Jim, when I realized who in the hell was calling me tonight, I thought for sure you wanted to come over and probably 'beat the hell out of me.' Little did I know it was really 'fuck the hell out of me!'

Shaking his head, Todd then said with one big smile on his face, "I have now fucked one hot Gary, and I have now also been fucked by one hot, Gary's dad! Come on man, let's go shower. I don't know if you know it or not, but I'm staying here for the night!

You supposedly, are out of town for the night, you've got a motel room all paid for, and besides, you've got me here too. It's too late for me to drive home, and, besides, you are too hunky of a guy to leave behind, and besides – I need to fuck that ass of yours in the morning, and maybe get some more of you, up in my ass too! OK?"

CHAPTER TEN:

And I Want Yours

"Jason, hon, I'm going over to Sherry's. Make sure you find out from that carpet guy exactly when they expect to come install the carpet. Make sure it's not next Tuesday. I've got the sorority meeting here that day. OK?"

"Yeah, OK Nancy. How long you planning on being gone?"

"Probably till about supper time. I'm helping Sherry with some new recipes she wants to fix for Dean, so probably until about then. You wanna go out for supper tonight since I'm gonna be gone?"

"Yeah, OK. Hey, tell Sherry I said, 'Hi,' and tell her to have Dean call me to see if he can play golf Saturday. Bye honey!"

"Well, she's finally gone." Jason said, after he watched her drive out of the front drive, and as he entered the bedroom where Todd was measuring. "Hey, when do you guys expect to be coming, to install the carpet – any idea?"

"Well, as far as I can tell right now, it should be next week, maybe Thursday or Friday. We need to make sure it gets here first, before we can do a firm scheduling. That OK?"

"Yeah, just don't plan on Tuesday. My wife just told me that day don't work."

As Todd looked up to reply to Jason's statement, he was very surprised to see that Jason was standing there and actually, very openly, rubbing his crotch! "Yeah – uh, we'll call and do the scheduling once it arrives, OK?"

Todd was rather un-nerved as he realized that Jason was not stopping his rubbing and was obviously wanting Todd to see what he was doing.

"My wife's gone for the afternoon. Wanna have some fun?"

Shocked, Todd replied, "What? What do you mean? What did you say!?"

"What I mean is – wanna play around some? I know you're into guys. Saw that gay mag laying in the back seat of your car when I came walking in beside it. You're a hot looking little stud, and I'm horny for some good tight ass, and from what I can see from here, you've got one!"

"Whoa, whoa. Uh – I'm working here! Hey man, you're hot and yeah, guess maybe I forgot to hide that mag, but sure didn't expect anybody to be looking in my car. Mr. Sampson, I like the idea, but I can't. I can't play around with customers, and besides, you're a married man!"

"Yeah, so I'm married, and you are working! So big deal! Come on man, let's go in the bedroom for just a little while. Then I'll help you finish measuring. Come on man, I need some ass and I want yours!"

Looking up at Jason, since Todd was down on the floor measuring the floor inside of a small closet, he took a good long gaze and liked what he saw. Jason was, in his thinking anyway, about 37 or 38, about 6 foot tall, a big chest, a small waist, looked to be in damn good athletic shape. That statement was becoming more and more obvious, since Jason was now almost naked. As he was strongly suggesting to Todd that they go into the bedroom, he had already removed his shirt – exposed one damn good pair of pecks, covered with a fine layer of light brown hair, and was now removing his pants – to expose one very big hard dick, that did not have any briefs hiding it! He was not waiting on Todd's acceptance before showing Todd just what was available for the taking. Jason's dick was stiff and hard, and it showed just how anxious Jason was for Todd's ass.

"Your name's Todd, right?"

"Yeah. Yeah, it is."

"Hey Todd, you want this don't you?" Jason asked as he flipped his dick back and forth directly in front of, and very close to, Todd's face.

Todd unknowingly licked his lips as he watched Jason's hardon flip back and forth.

"Come on man, come on! Let's go in the bedroom and have some fun. You know as well as I do, you want this. I can see it in your eyes! Come on. It's just you and me. It won't take us long. Hey, so I'm married. Doing her just ain't as much fun as doing somebody like you! Come on man! I need that butt of yours for a few minutes, come on!"

Todd continued to sit there and continued to ponder just what he should do. His smarter side told him to just keep working, and his hornier side told him to go for it. Looking at Jason and the body he was now fully showing, was making it damn hard to turn him down.

"But what if she comes back home for some reason? We could get caught!"

"No, we'll go down to the basement workroom. We can fuck down there. Besides, I got some vice grips down there and I like for guys to put 'em on my tits for me. Willing? Wanta to do that for me? I like to feel them pinching my tits and hanging there. They feel so fucking good and I like for guys to put 'em on me. I can put 'em on myself, but it just plan feels better if some other guy puts 'em on me. Come on Todd, come on!"

The mere idea of clamping some vice grips onto Jason's tits was way too much for Todd to turn down. That was the clincher!

"Really? Really you want me to clamp some vice grips on you? Is that what you said?"

"Yeah! Yes I did! Oh yeah man, cause that feels so fucking good! I love it and I love having guys doing that to me! Come on man, let's go!"

Still not being so sure he was doing the right thing, Todd got up and followed Jason, and his tight solid bare ass down the stairs, and into the basement.

Once in the basement, Jason then led them through another door into a small room that he referred to as the workroom. "Hey, this is my workroom. Won't tell you what type of work I usually do in here, but it kind of looks like a workroom, right?"

Looking around, Todd answered, "Uh, yeah! Yeah looks like a workroom, but that's not what you usually use it for?"

"No hell no! Now listen, this is just between you and me, and for God's sake, don't let Nancy know any of this, but this is more for what you and I are gonna do in here than for any work. Hey, the tools are all for show. Except for the vice grips and those polished poles over there. Once in awhile when my dick just ain't long enough to suit some guy, so those poles come in handy! Come here man, let me pull those pants of yours down and get that cute little butt of yours out here so I can do my thing in it! My dick is good and hard and real ready to do some good pounding in that ass!"

Jason moved Todd over toward the workbench, and unfastened his belt and the buttons on his pants. He pulled both the pants and Todd's briefs down just far enough so that by laying Todd over the top of the workbench, his bare ass was now standing out there for Jason's admiration and use! Jason reached up into a cupboard and pulled out a small can of Crisco and fingered some up into Todd's butt! Todd could then feel the tip of Jason's meat head hit the rose bud of his ass.

"Oh yeah, yeah, yeah that feels good! Yeah, do me!"

"Oh shit man, you have got one tight little asshole back here man – it is tight! Man that is making my dick really feel good. Damn man, you have been fucked before, right?"

Letting his head rather hang down as he truly enjoyed the feel of Jason forcing his thick dick up into the narrow hole, Todd uttered, "Yeah. Yeah I have – some. Not too much yet – but yeah. Hey man, your dick feels good back there, you doing OK?"

"Hell yeah, I'm doing OK, if you are. Seriously man, I'm filling your asshole up a hell of a lot more than any of the other guys

I've rammed it up into. You sure you're OK and not hurting too much?"

"No, I'm OK. God yes man – I can tell you've got my ass filled, though! I can tell that! It's full and yeah, of course it hurt some, just pushing that damn thing up in me is of course gonna hurt me some, but I guess I like the hurt. Just keep pushing man, keep pushing! I want to know I took all of it! Yeah, man, it's feeling good going up in there!"

"OK man, OK! You want the rest of it? You want all of it?"

"Yeah, yeah, yeah! Yeah man push it up in me. Yeah it's feeling good ram me! Ram my ass!"

With that instruction, Jason did! He rammed Todd's ass with one major shove and a ramming push!

"Ouch! Oh shit man – oh shit! Oh God man, oh shit! Oh God, I've got it all now, don't I? I've got it all!" Todd just almost screamed – loud!

Suddenly from across the room, Jason and Todd heard, "Jason, what in the fucking hell is going on in here? Jason, what in the hell is happening!? You fucking him!? You fucking that guy?"

Instantly, and without warning, Jason pulled his dick out of Todd's ass, and immediately turned around to find his kid brother standing there in the doorway.

"Jason, what in the hell are you doing? Who's that?"

"Oh shit Dean, where in the hell did you come from? How long you been standing there?"

"Well, just for a second, but definitely long enough to see you ramming that pole of yours up in that guy's ass! What in the hell is going on here? Jason, are you fucking this guy? Shit man, you are totally fucking naked! Jason, what in the hell man! What in the hell is going on here? You are fucking some guy down here in your basement? When did you start doing this?"

"Hey Dean, cool man, cool! Hey, I just wanted some ass, and this guy was measuring for the carpet and I saw a gay mag in the back seat of his car, and since Nancy was over at your place helping Sherry, I decided to take advantage of him. That's all man, that's all. Just some quick ass and a quick shoot off. Really man, it's no big deal!"

"So this is really what you built this room for, uh? Gay sex sessions! You know Jason, when you built this little room down here, I really wondered just why in the hell. I thought, you know, ole Jason really don't need some special work place down there – now I know why! Look at the stuff you've got hanging around handy down here. Chains, ropes, some wood that kind of looks more like paddles to me, some stuff stashed in the doors and drawers I assume? Just what would I find if I opened some of these doors? Dildo? Butt plugs? Hey, looks like I don't have to look for the Crisco do I? Everything's good and handy – right big brother, right?"

Todd had quickly stood up and turned around after Jason so quickly removed himself from Todd's ass, and he was now standing there listening to the excited and confused interchange between the two brothers. It was very obvious to Todd that Dean knew nothing about his older brother's interests and desires of fucking a guy's ass. As he stood there, he questioned immediately if he should try and pull his briefs and his pants back up and try and make a run for it, or just stay cool and see if everything was gonna be OK between the two brothers. Being as scared and alarmed as he was right then, Todd questioned how in the world could he even slightly hope that everything was gonna be OK – just because he now, found Dean to be even a hotter looking guy than his older brother was. Todd thought, "How in the hell can I even think about wanting to play with Dean, when this whole situation could get very, very nasty between these two brothers, and I would be right in the very middle of it? How in the hell can I lust over some guy that just might blow his top over this whole situation of just finding his brother fucking my ass? How in the hell can I even think that way?"

"So who is this guy, anyway? Where'd you find him?"

"Hey Dean, he was measuring the house for the carpet. He's just the guy from the carpet store. I'm the one that suggested this! I saw his mag in the car, I looked at his ass when he was bending over upstairs, and I got horny man, I got horny. Come on Dean, haven't you and your buddies ever fucked some guy's ass before? Come on man, I'm sure you guys have fucked some guy somewhere, sometime, haven't you?"

Todd was listening to this interchange between the two brothers, Jason, fully nude, but no longer showing a hardon, and the younger brother Dean, that Todd was wishing was fully nude, and showing whatever he was carrying in his pants. He could not fail to imagine just how great it would be to get a chance at the younger brother and his dick, or his ass, or any part of that body that Todd could touch and feel! He guessed Dean to be maybe 33 or 34, and just like his brother at least six feet tall, and obviously a person that has spent his share of time in a gym with the heavier weights held above his head, and from what Todd could see, a crotch that promised good things! As Todd looked at it, even during his fears of not knowing just how much trouble was still gonna happen down here, he kept wishing for just a small chance to see just what was packed inside of that crotch. It looked full, and it made Todd wish for it, and want it!

"Hey Jason, let's not worry about me right now! How often you get guys down here, in your little playroom, as I now understand what is really is for? What once a month, once a week, everyday? Yeah, just how often you get to use this place?"

"Hey Dean, knock it off man, knock it off! No fucking big deal man, no fucking big deal! Yeah, I like ass! Good solid strong ass! Ass like this guy's got! How in the hell did you get down here anyway? I didn't know you were even here?"

"Hey, I came into the house and couldn't find you anyplace, and since your car was outside, and the other car too, I figured you were around here someplace, so I decided maybe downstairs in the – oh yeah – workroom! Hell man, by the time I hit the bottom step I knew something funny and different was going on down here. I don't know just how fucking big that dick of yours is when it's good and hard, but from the way you were making this poor guy scream, it must be a fucking ass full."

Then looking directly at Todd, Dean asked, "You OK kid? You OK? You were screaming pretty good when he fucked you, you OK?"

Todd looked at Dean and answered, "Oh yeah! Yeah I'm fine! I know I kind of yelled louder than I should have, and it did hurt for a moment when he finally slammed it up in me, but yeah I'm OK.

Thanks for asking though! Hey, please don't blame your brother for
this! Really, I could have told him no, but I like to get fucked in the
ass, and hell, look at him! If you knew you liked to get fucked in
the ass and some guy that looks like him, or like you too, asked if he
could fuck you, do you think you could turn either one of you guys
down? Hell no! Hey man, he was not all to blame. I agreed. Don't
be mad at him, I sure ain't!"

"Well, hell no! I'm sure you ain't mad at him. You're the one
getting fucked by him. If you like getting fucked of course you aren't
mad."

Now, getting probably more courage than he even realized
that he had, Todd looked at Dean and asked, "You ever fucked some
guy's ass before?"

"Yeah, have you?" Jason quickly entered. "I asked you, but
you never gave me an answer! Now Todd's asking, you ever fucked
some guy's ass?"

Very lowly, very softly and quite calmly Dean replied, "Yeah
once. Yeah, once but only once."

"Oh so little brother has fucked some guy before then,
right?"

Quietly, Dean replied, "Yeah, but like I said – only once!"

"So little brother tell me about it, tell me the how, the where
and the when. See, fucking some guy's ass ain't so weird and unusual
is it? You done it before, haven't you?"

"Yeah, once! Just once!"

"Well, – so tell me bout it brother, tell me! Who, when and all
the good stuff!"

"Hey it was like maybe two years ago. Mike and I were out
on patrol, and stupid Mike backed into some guy's car in the parking
lot of a restaurant. We knew we were gonna be in big trouble with the
department if it had to get reported, even though it didn't do anything
to the cruiser. We talked to the guy that was driving and he knew
we were gonna have trouble if they reported it, so we made them a
deal."

"Them? Wait, them? Who's the them?

"OK! Him and some other guy that was with him."

"OK, a deal! What deal? Shit man, this is getting good! OK Dean, what was the deal?"

"We asked them if there was anything that maybe we could do for them to keep them from reporting it since it was so minor and we agreed we'd pay for the repair, too. We didn't think about them maybe being gay guys. They talked for a minute and then they told us that if we'd each fuck each of them, we didn't even need to pay for the repair, since they said they didn't think they'd be getting it fixed anyway. They said, just a quick fuck, and if it was OK with us, maybe suck on our dicks for a second or two so they could proudly proclaim that they had each been fucked by a cop and had each sucked on a cop. They said if we'd agree to that, they totally forget about the little accident and never report it."

"Well, shit man, what a fucking deal! Sorry for the pun! What a fucking deal! So I assume, you and Mike went for it then, right?"

"Yeah, we agreed we'd fuck each of 'em, and let 'em suck on us, if they'd forget about reporting the accident. His car wasn't really hurt hardly any, anyway, and Mike and I sure didn't want it getting reported to the department, so we agreed to do it. We looked at each other and kind of agreed, 'Hey, what the hell, it's their asses not ours, could be fun!' We agreed neither one of us had ever done this before, and hell, maybe it was our time to find out what some guy's ass felt like with our dicks stuck up in it, and maybe shooting off up there, too."

"Oh so little brother fucks a couple of guys in exchange for them keeping their mouths shut about the car thing, right? I got that right?"

"Yeah, yeah, you got it right. But that was the only time!"

"Yeah, but wait here a minute! You told us you only fucked once. What you mean is you only fucked once, but you fucked two guys that time, right?"

"Yeah, right."

"Well, so tell me! How was it? You got sucked off, too?"

With this interchange going on, Todd was starting to get his hopes up that maybe Jason was starting to get his kid brother, who, it was now apparent, was either a city policeman or a state trooper, to maybe open up a little and hopefully – oh yes Todd thought, "Hopefully, Hopefully," would want to fuck another ass – again. Again and real soon! Todd was fully hoping that maybe 'older brother' was really into getting 'little brother' to join them, so that he couldn't say anything about his brother's actions down in the basement!

"So, tell me. I mean tell us, how'd it go? You fuck those guys? Get blown off by those guys?"

"Yeah, yeah, yeah! Yeah, we fucked and they sucked!"

"So little brother, just how was it? Good? Like it?"

"Yeah, yeah, yeah! Yeah it was good. Yes, I admit it was good. I'd never fucked a solid tight ass like that before, and yeah, I liked it. Felt good pushing on something real solid and firm. The one guy, he liked it real rough I guess, cause he kept yelling for me to slam him harder. That was the first time I'd ever been fucking when she, well this time it was a he, he was screaming for me to slam him harder. That was different. And yeah, it felt good. I guess that's what you were doing to this guy when I came in wasn't it?"

"Then looking at Todd, Dean asked, "You like it rough and hard too? You like that guy I fucked that night? You like it slammed up in you real hard too?"

"Yeah, yes I do! Yeah the rougher the guy can do me, the better I like it. Your brother was doing me real good before we had to stop. He was slamming me good!"

"So I kind of guess what you are saying is, you want him to get back in you and slam you some more, right?"

"Oh yeah, really, yeah. Please, but, if you liked doing that other guy that night, I'd like for you to use me too, and see if my ass feels just as good as his did! I'd like that! I want you to slam my ass too!"

Then looking at Jason, Todd asked, "Is that OK? Is it OK if he fucks me too? I mean if he wants to. I really wish he would, I'd love to have both of you guys fucking me. Please!?"

As Jason looked over toward his brother to ask if he was interested, he realized that Dean was standing there and unconsciously rubbing his crotch.

"Well, little brother, from what I see you doing, I guess I really don't need to ask you if you want to join in or not! Kind of looks to me like you're supporting a woody as we talk about how some guys like it good and rough in his ass. Come on Dean, strip down. Let's fuck this guy and make all of us happy! You've fucked a guy before, well – really as I now understand it, two guys, and so this ain't gonna be nothing new for you, just giving you the chance to do it again."

"Oh shit man, shit! I shouldn't be doing this, I shouldn't!"

"So why not? Hey man, all of us guys need sex as much and as often as we can get it, and so once in awhile it's some guys ass instead of our wives. Loosen up Dean, I'm not gonna tell anybody! Come on man, get your clothes off."

Then turning Todd back around toward the workbench so that he could continue his previously interrupted fucking session, Jason asked Todd, "Hey man. You like to suck cock too? Since I'm gonna be fucking your cute little ass back here, how about if we get Dean to jump up there on the workbench and while I fuck your ass, you can suck his dick. You'll like his dick – little brother's got a big dick! Wanna do that?"

As Todd was truly trying to turn around far enough to watch Dean get undressed, so he could see what Jason was taking about when he mentioned Dean's dick, he exclaimed, "Oh yes! God yes! Yeah man that sounds great!"

Dean finished getting undressed and following his brother's suggestion, he jumped up on the workbench and spread his legs around Todd's upper body so that Todd could place his face right in Dean's crotch.

As Dean was moving into position, Todd let out an, "Oh my God! Oh shit, what a fucking dick you've got man! What a fucking dick! Oh God I hope I can swallow all of that! Man oh live! Oh Dean man, what did those guys say the night you fucked them with this dick? Oh shit could they take it?"

As Dean positioned himself right in front of Todd's mouth, and aimed his nine and a half inch dick into Todd's mouth, he replied, "Well, one of them took it pretty good, but the other guy, he had a lot of trouble. He told me he had never had one that big stuck up his asshole before, so it took him some time to take it. Got to admit, today, that's kind of one of my curiosities. I want to see if you can take it OK or not. That other guy that night, he took it pretty good, but he made some comments about how big it was too. I guess maybe I just never realized that maybe it is bigger than most guy's."

"Holy shit man!" Jason entered. "My God Dean! Ever since you've been a little guy, all of us older guys have always made comments about how much bigger you are than the rest of us. Haven't you ever wondered why guys always wanted to go skinny-dipping with you. Shit man, they all wanted to see that dick of yours. Seriously man, with the dick you've got, I'm surprised that you don't have it stuck down some guy's mouth all the time. Seriously man, don't other guys make comments or approach you, like maybe, when you're in the restroom taking a piss? Come on man, I'm sure other guys make comments, don't they?"

"Yeah, yeah they do – once in a while." Dean replied as he felt rather cornered to be honest since his older brother was being honest about how the older guys had always wanted to see his dick and was jealous of its size. "Yeah, I've had some guys that asked me if they could suck it."

"Really, really Dean? Some guys have asked you if they could suck it?" Jason asked, as he continued his slamming and ramming of Todd's ass, and as Todd managed an inch at a time of getting more and more of that dick down and into his mouth! "Come on man, tell me, tell me about getting asked. Ever let any of 'em suck you off?"

"Yeah, hell yeah I guess I might just as well be honest with you now that you already know about Mike and me fucking those two guys. And, as I sit here with about three fourths of it stuck down this guy's throat. Yeah, I get asked a lot when in a public restroom, unless I've got my uniform on. I've never had anyone ask when I'm in uniform. I sure have watched a lot of guys that I thought maybe were gonna, but nobody ever did. I'm not sure what I'd do if I was in uniform and a guy asked. Guess it'd depend on what he looked like and what my mood was."

"So man, how often do guys try to hit you up?"

"Oh, probably a couple of times a month. If I'm out of uniform, of course, that's when I get offers."

"Hey brother, ever have another officer hit up on you? Ever let another cop take it from you?"

"Yeah, once in Atlanta at an officers convention. He knew I was a cop too, but he told me that we were from different towns, and my dick was just too fucking hot to leave alone, and he asked me to come up to his room with him, and he told me all I had to do was stand there, and let him suck. I figured hell, I hadn't had any sex for about five days anyway, and it was gonna be another three days before I got home, so I decided getting a blow job was better than just jerking it off! So yeah, I went! And I was damn glad I did! He was one fucking good sucker. I swear he could have made a living being a professional sucker! At one time I thought he was gonna suck my whole body down his throat."

"God man, he must have been good! You cum for him?"

"Hell yes I did! I even went back to his room the next day and asked him to do it again.

"Oh shit man! Dean you and me talking about guys asking you if they can suck you off is really turning me on. I am just about ready to unload all of my cum up in this kid's ass. I am so fucking turned on right now that I am about to explode! Todd you ready man, you ready? I'm gonna load you, I'm gonna load you! Oh shit man – I'm cummin' man, I'm cummmin' man!"

"Oh God Jason, I'm cumming too! Jason I'm loading him too! Oh shit man, oh God I just let everything fly! Hey guy, you OK? Oh Jason – I didn't known I was so close, but I guess when I started telling you about that cop in Atlanta, I guess that got me all hot 'n bothered, and besides, I think this guy started sucking on me stronger then too! Hey, you OK? Hey kid, you OK?"

Not wanting to take his mouth off of the cop's enormous dick, Todd managed to shake his head "Yes" and utter a small "Yeah." It wasn't until then, at that time, that Todd finally realized that Dean obviously did not know what his name was, and he had been referring to him as "Kid." Suddenly that was a hot turn on to him. He liked that! He realized that he was hardly any younger than Dean was, but the fact that Dean was calling him the "Kid" was a major, for Todd. It made him feel like he was taking care of, maybe his "Daddy," or at least someone quite a bit older. He liked it!

"Oh shit man, that took it out of me!" Jason announced as he leaned forward onto Todd's back and rested there for a minute. "Man, I have not shot off that hard in months and months. I guess this tight little solid ass and the way we were talking about you getting sucked off in Atlanta really make me do it! Shit man, I'm fucking exhausted! How you doing Dean? How's he doing on that dick of your?"

"Oh shit man, he is doing great! This kid knows how to suck a cock! I mean it! I think he comes in a close second to that cop in Atlanta that did me. I don't know how long this guy's been sucking dick, but he must have started as a young kid. He sure knows how! Damn that felt good!"

"Well, hey man. He wanted you to fuck his ass today. You gonna be able to do that since you came already?"

"Well, as far as I'm concerned, I'm still willing. Hey Kid, you still want me to fuck that butt of yours?"

Still sucking and not being willing to pull off of Dean's dick until he had to, Todd emphatically nodded "Yes," and attempted to rather yell "Yes."

"Hey he wants it! You gonna come up here and let him suck on you while I do his ass? Feel up to that?"

"Yeah, I can do that. I kind of think he probably already has figured out I've already cum once, so I doubt I'd do that again, but if he wants to suck me, I'm sure willing."

The two brother switched places, and after Jason cleaned his dick off so that Todd did not need to suck on shit juices and Crisco, he positioned himself on the workbench and let Todd take his dick into his mouth.

As Jason took ahold of the sides of Todd's head and aimed his dick in, he said, "Hey guy, not as big as little brother's, but it's all I got."

Even though Todd had his mouth full of a dick that was totally hard and stiff again already, Todd managed to utter, "Big enough, big enough! It's big!"

Dean positioned himself back at Todd's rear door and as Todd was taking Jason's rod into his mouth, Dean said, "Hang on Kid, here it comes!"

Getting one dick stuffed down his throat from one end, and then taking Dean's pole, all in one push, up the other end, almost raised Todd up off of the floor! He uttered an, "Oh man, oh man!"

Both Dean and Jason asked him at the same time if he was OK. Just as emphatically as he could, Todd indicated a very big, "Yeah, oh God yes! Fuck me men – fuck me!"

That was a very clear indication to both of the brothers that Todd was definitely getting what he wanted, and that made both men go after him with vim and vigor! Dean started fucking his ass like he had never fucked before. "Oh my God man! Oh my God this is great! You OK kid? You OK?" He literally yelled as he pounded Todd's ass like a fucking sledge hammer going in and out!

"Oh shit man!" Jason was almost yelling. "Oh shit man! I didn't think I'd get all excited again after I just came, but hang on Todd, I'm gonna cum, oh man – I'm gonna cum! Oh here it comes man, here it comes! Here it is – I'm cummmmmmin', man – I'm cummmmin' again!

"Oh shit man! Oh man, I'm cumin too! Hey Kid, get ready, I'm about ready to load you back here again! I'm gonna mix my cum with brother's cum, and you're gonna have some of both of us up in there! Hang on man, here it comes! Oh man – I'm cummmmin, oh yeah, I'm cummmmin!"

Todd realized that he was now the center character of a gay story that could not be written. Of all of the gay stuff he had read so far, he realized that no person in any story could have lived the experiences that he was getting that day, in that basement 'workroom', as it was called. Two fucking hot brothers, and one a cop that any gay guy would jump off of a cliff for, had just taken him, and used him, from both ends, and had used him for all he was worth. Each man had loaded him both in the mouth and in the ass! He laid there with his face in Jason's bare lap, and with Dean spread out across his back, still with Dean's oversized dick stuck up in his ass, and he realized that what he had just experienced was, way beyond, what any normal gay guy could ever hope to experience during any of his lifetime. Todd knew that when he left that house that day, he'd be taking a hell of a lot more with him than just the room measurements! He was taking some of Jason, and he was taking some of Dean. And he was taking memories that could never be duplicated! As he was walked out of that basement, that day, he felt like he was not only himself, but partly Jason, and partly Dean, too! And he liked the feeling – immensely! He knew he could measure up with the big boys now, really, in a very big way!

CHAPTER ELEVEN:

"I Had No Idea, No Idea At All!"

"Brian, Brian, you in here?" Todd hollered into the restroom of the carpet warehouse where he and Brian were picking up a load of carpet.

"Brian, you in here?" Todd again hollered as he entered the restroom and went around the corner to see if Brian was there. He had lost Brian, and since the truck was now ready to get loaded, he was trying to find him so Brian could check the order and make sure the right stuff was loaded.

Going into the restroom and rather checking out the floor of the four stalls, Todd finally found some feet in the last stall. "Brian, that you? The truck's ready to get loaded. Come on!"

"Hey Todd, I'll be right there, give me a minute."

"Well, hurry up, I need you out at the truck!"

As Todd stood there for only a moment, rather wishing Brian could hurry up a little, something very weird seemed to be going on. Suddenly Todd realized that Brian was not in that stall alone. He just saw two additional feet hit the floor, and those feet were facing Brian!

"Brian open the door! Open the door!"

With Todd's hand on the handle, pulling the door toward himself, so that once it was unlocked from the inside, it would come open, it suddenly did!

Pulling the door open, Todd looked inside of the stall to find Brian seated on the toilet, and an additional man, somebody he did not know, standing there, facing Brian, with his pants down to his knees. Brian's pants were down to his ankles, but rightfully so, since he was the one in the position to use the toilet, if anybody intended to.

"What in the hell is going on in here?" Todd firmly asked as he looked at both Brian, his 22 year old, co-worker – the former high school football star, and then the additional occupant of the stall – a stud, of unknown name right then, but none the less, still a definitely hot, hot, looking stud! A man of about age 40 or 41, about six foot tall, and a guy that definitely had the build and the looks of somebody that was either an athlete or must have been the owner of a workout gym someplace. And, a stud with a stick that was just as definitely as admirable as all of the rest of him. And, a stick that was still hard, looking very, very, hard!

"What's this? What's going on in here?" Todd asked as he managed to look the man over. He didn't allow any emotions to show, but he sure did like what he saw! The body and the dick, both!

"I don't know!" Brian answered. "Todd, I don't know! He came in here when I came in, and he told me he wanted to get sucked off. I don't know who he is. He made me do it!"

"So guy, what's your name?"

"Hey man, what difference does it make to you who I am. I didn't tell him I wanted to get sucked off! He asked me if I wanted him to give me a blow job, I said 'Yeah,' and I was taking it till you came in."

"Hey Brian, go on out to the truck, get our order sheet out of the cab and check what they're loading. Make sure we get the right stuff! I want to talk to this guy for a minute! I'll be out in just a minute! I want to see just what he has to say about this."

Brian quickly stood up, grabbed his pants, pulled them up and headed out of the restroom and toward the truck.

After Brian left the room, Todd looked at the man and asked. "Wait here just a minute! He asked to give you a blow job, right? Is that what you're saying? He's the one that brought it up?"

"Yeah, I am! I was in the hall and when he walked by, he looked at me and just asked, 'Want sucked off?' Then he ginned and nodded toward the restroom. I figured hey, why not! And he would have finished if you hadn't walked in!"

"So where you from? You from out of town too? You here picking up carpet too or something?"

"Yeah. I figured what the hell, I'm from out of town. I figured he's from out of town, so I figured, go for it! You his boss or something?"

"No, I'm not his boss, just a co-worker! One that did not know my co-worker was quite that available!"

"What you mean, that available? Sounds to me like maybe you'd take care of that mouth of his too, if you had known it was available! That what you mean?"

"Yeah, I kinda guess that's what I'm saying. I had no idea, no idea at all!" Then sticking his hand out for a handshake, Todd added, "Hi, I'm Todd Underwood. Got to admit, I sure do like the looks of that rod you got there! You let many guys get to it like that?"

Extending his hand out for a hand shake, he replied, "Hi, I'm John Benson. And hell yeah, as often as possible! You're kinda drooling over it yourself! Wanna finish what your buddy started?"

"Yeah, I wanna do one quick suck – just enough to taste it and feel it in my mouth, but I'm afraid somebody might come in and catch us – so let me do it real quick!"

After about an hour's worth of silent riding back toward home base, Todd finally said, "OK Brian, let's talk about it, OK?"

"No, I really don't want to! He lied! He said I asked him, and he was the one that said he wanted me to do it when I came into the restroom, and I know you believe him, and not me, so no, I don't want to talk about it! Forget it, just do me a favor and don't tell anybody back home what I did, please? I don't want everybody thinking I go around sucking off guy's cocks, OK?"

"Hey Brian, I need to tell you something!"

Rather angrily, Brian asked, "Yeah – what?"

"I sucked him too!"

"You what!? You sucked him too!? Todd, you shitting me man!?"

"No, no I'm not! My greatest shock, when I found you in there with him, was that I had no idea you were up to that, or let me tell you – I'd had you doing me a long time ago! Yeah, after I sent you out to check the order and be with the truck, I admitted to him that I did not know you did guys and then he asked me if I wanted to suck it too, and I thought, hell yeah, man! The dick he was swinging there, hell yeah!"

"Todd you're kidding me, right? You really sucked on him? Did you?"

"Hey Brian, I'm not gonna lie to you about something like that! I finally decided I needed to tell you, so you'd know I'm sure not going back to the company and tell everybody what went on back there. Yeah, I will admit, at first I thought maybe I'd just keep it a secret, that I did him too, but after thinking it through, I finally decided that I'd be a total fool if I hid it from you – that I do guys, cause man, if you're into it too, I want some time with you – if you agree!"

"Oh shit man, please Todd, please don't be lying to me! Please Todd, you're not starting to just making fun of me are you? Please Todd, don't lie to me!"

As Todd reached down with his left hand, grabbed and then jerked on his crotch, he looked at Brian with a very wide grin, and he continued, "No Brian, no lie! I've looked at you before, and I've looked at you in a lot of different ways – so to say – and I will admit, I'm glad this happened today! If you're willing, I want us to spend some good private time together as soon as we can, OK?"

"Yeah we can, yeah! Oh Todd I can't believe this! When you caught me in the restroom with that guy, I thought I was dead. I figured you'd go back to the company and tell 'em what happened, and then I'd just plain get fired. Oh man, thank god that's not gonna happen, is it? I mean, you're not gonna tell anybody, right?"

"Hey guy, you think I'm gonna go back and tell everybody I found you sucking on some big dick in a restroom, then I chased you out so I could suck on it, and then have him stick it up in my ass for a second?"

"You what? What did you say? Todd, did he fuck you too?"

Grinning rather "smirkishly", Todd answered. "Yeah, but just for a minute or two! I sucked on him, and while I was doing that, he just said, 'Oh man, I'd love to see what this feels like rammed up in your butt!' I didn't say a thing. I just stood up, pulled my pants down, spit some saliva on my hand, smeared it on my ass, and bent over, grabbed the toilet bowl and he put it up in me! Wow! What a great feeling! I kind of guess he liked it too! He grabbed my waist and in just about 45 seconds, he was giving me the cum he had planned for you! Sorry bout that man! I got it up in my butt instead of you getting it down the throat. Got to admit, I'm starting to feel pretty guilty of interrupting you and him. Guess I gotta make that up to you somehow now!"

"Hey man, from what I'm starting to find out about you now, which I of course never knew before, there is gonna be plenty of chances for you to make that up to me! I will make damn sure of it. God man, I can't believe this! Todd, I've watched you for a long time now, and I've wanted to play with you but hell man, I sure as hell never guessed you for one of the guys that would do it! Oh yeah man, yeah, we're gonna have some good times together. Yeah, I want at that body of yours man, yeah I do!"

Looking over toward Brian, Todd grinned a big grin and said, "Good, I'm sure glad to hear that!"

"Hey, I sure as hell never knew that you played around with guys, and I sure as hell never even thought of you as maybe a guy that even thinks about it! Damn man, I might have been missing out of some good stuff here. Hell, it's not, might have been – I know damn well I have been missing out! Shit man, there have been so many times when I just wanted to grab you and strip you to see what you've got in there! Damn man, wish I could have watched that guy fuck your butt! Shit man, that would have been a real turn on for me! Todd, how often you play around with guys?"

"Not a lot, I guess. Well, maybe as often as I can. See, I just started doing the gay stuff not too long ago. I wanted to for a long time, but it was just a few months ago I finally got something going. See – now if I had known about you, you could have taught me what I wanted to know a long time ago."

"Oh shit man, I wish I had known too! Todd, I've always thought you were a hot looking guy. I'd have done you a long time ago. Oh man, I can't believe this! Hey Todd, there's a roadside rest up here about another ten or 15 miles. What do you think of the idea of pulling in there and if it's not busy, letting me see your dick and maybe sucking on it some – OK?"

"I'm game man, I'm game!"

Moments later, "Hey five miles more! You see that sign Todd?"

"Yeah, sure did Brian! I been watching for it just as much as you have been. I've been sitting here with a ragging hardon ever since you suggested we stop here. Hope like hell it's empty and nobody's here. Hey, know what we ought to do?"

"What? What'd you mean? What you talking about Todd?"

"That guy you were sucking off in the restroom? His name is John Benson. After I sucked on him for a minute and then he stuck it up my ass for a second or two, we discovered we both live south, down I-65, he lives down in Tennessee, and so we decided to exchange cell phone numbers just in case we happen to get kind of close again sometime, and I think we ought to call him and see where he's at right now. Interested? If he's pretty close here, might be fun to see if he'll stop for a few minutes, what you say?"

"I say hell yes! Shit yeah! I want some more of that dick if possible! How'd he feel up in your ass? He's pretty big, ain't he?"

"Yeah it's big and it felt damn good! If we can get him to stop, you wanna see if you can get fucked by him?"

"Hell yes! Shit yes! Call him and see where he's at. See if he's close by here or not!"

Todd pulled the truck into the roadside rest area and expressed his pleasure that it was almost totally empty. There were only two trucks in the truck section, and only about four family cars over in the car section.

Todd made the call to John, and then reported to Brian. Hey man – good news! I kind of think, real good news anyway! How you feel about staying in Indianapolis over night?"

"What? Do what? Why?"

"He's already got a motel room reserved in Indianapolis. He didn't plan on driving back, all today. He's by himself, and he said he don't like to push it too much, so he's stopping in Indianapolis for the night and then going on home tomorrow morning. He wants us to come and stay with him at the motel? What you think? You know damn well it's not sleep he's thinking of! It's sex, man, it's sex! He told me he's horny for some of both of us! And you heard me tell him how I wanted to taste that rod again, didn't you? What you think?"

"Yeah man, but what we gonna tell the company? We can't just come in about 18 hours late and act like nothing happened!"

"No, I'm gonna call and tell Tom that we got a late start back, and instead of driving after dark, we decided we wanted to just stay someplace in Indy and finish the drive tomorrow. We don't have any installations scheduled for tomorrow anyway, so if we don't get home till bout noon, no big deal. I'll just tell him that since this was our idea, we'll pay for the room and it won't cost the company anything for us to stay over. What you think?"

"Do it man, do it! Yeah, let's do it! You gotta call that John guy back and find out where, and tell him we're gonna do it?"

"Yeah, I gotta call him, and then I'll call Tom and tell him we'll be home tomorrow. You need to call anybody and tell them you won't be home tonight?"

"Yeah, I need to call Shane and let him know. He's my lover, but I never mention him around the company or anybody from there."

"Oh shit man, what's he gonna think about you doing this? This gonna piss him off?"

"Hey, you ain't gonna tell Tom the real reason we're staying over are you?"

"No, no, of course not!"

"Well, same thing with Shane! I'll tell him later. Beside, he needs to find out about you sometime anyway, since I want a three-way with the three of us. Me, you and him! What you think?"

"He hot as you? Well, – he don't need to be, but just the idea of getting in bed with two like you, is a major fucking turn on to me! Sounds hot as hell! Yeah, of course I want to! Fuck yes!"

Todd made the required calls, the one to John and the one to the company. They decided to just hang tight there at the roadside rest since Todd found out that John was behind them on I-65, and he should be able to join them at the rest stop in about 45 minutes or so.

Tom at the company told Todd that he was glad they were staying overnight, since they were having a very nasty rain storm, and he was glad Todd would not be driving in it. Tom was glad they were staying over, but it was for a totally different reason, than why Todd was so glad!

Brian called his partner Shane and reported in about the layover. As he got off the phone, he looked at Todd and said, "Well, that sure as the hell did not upset Shane any! I already knew he had been wanting to go spend the night with Coach Frank anyway, and he told me that he was gonna see if he could do that tonight, since I won't be home. Coach Frank is a hunk of a body that we met about six months ago, and we visit back and forth all the time now, but neither one of us have hit the hay, so to say, with him yet. So anyway, Shane is really hoping he can go visit him for the night. Sex! I can just see those two in the bed together. Well, as long as they stay in the bed. Knowing Shane and Coach both, they will probably be out of the bed and fucking on the floor within probably ten minutes. Both of those guys are like wild bores when they get active. Well, anyway that's what coach has told us, and as far as Shane goes, I know from first hand experience you need to almost wear body armor when playing with him!"

"God he sounds like fun! Yeah, now I really do want a three-way with you two. You get active like he does?"

"Well, I don't think I do! He tells me I get pretty wild, but I don't know. Guess maybe you'll have to find out for yourself, won't you?"

"Yeah, I will and I like the idea! I'm finding out pretty fast, I like sex more on the rougher side and not the 'willow-mellow' way. I can have that with Julie."

"Hey, I've been wanting to ask you bout that – now that I found out you play the guy thing. She know you're doing guys? You told her?"

"No, I ain't told her, but I think she's starting to get ideas something is not quite right. I'm not begging for sex anymore like I used to. She's even asked me once or twice if I was doing it with somebody else, and then she kind of laughed and accused me of probably doing it with some guy! I really had to bite my tongue then from telling her the truth. I guess the day will be here pretty soon when I'll have to be upfront and honest and tell her! I'm telling you Brian, sex with her just ain't the same anymore. Getting a chance to play with you tonight has got me all turned on and flustered, but the idea of being back in bed with her again, is just not exciting. I've found my true desires, and know it! How bout you? Ever fucked a gal?"

"Yeah, once! Only once! I was drunk as hell, and some other gay guys bet me fifty bucks I wouldn't fuck this gal that was at one of the dance clubs. So I wanted to show them, and so yeah I did! I was real sorry later! To me it was not worth the fifty bucks! I think I drank up the fifty bucks later that night just trying to forget what I had done. We did it out in the back seat of the car, and I swear after we got done, she told every person in the club I had just fucked her! Man, I was embarrassed! Now, if it had been one of the hot guys that was there that night, then I'd have never cared! And there were some damn hot looking guys in that club that night! I've always wished I'd taken some guy out and fucked him, just to see what his girlfriend would have said! Never went back to that club after that night! Decided I needed to just stay where the guys were at!"

Just then, Todd stated, "Hey Brian, here comes John!"

John pulled in, parked his truck, climbed out and said, "Hello men, how you doing?"

"Hey John, pretty good! Now better since you're here too, though! Like I told you on the phone, Brian and I are really looking forward to this! Thanks man, thanks! Like I told you earlier today, I had no idea about Brian being a guy's, guy, and of course he didn't know anything about me either, so ever since we kind of cleared the air, we've both been anxious to get at each other. Until you suggested our staying over for the night, I was really wondering just how soon he and I were gonna be able to make a connection. Now the idea of he and I, and you too, you sure can't ask for anything better than that, right Brian?"

"Right you are man! John – glad to actually meet you! We never really met earlier today. Kind of got to really know each other, but never even exchanged names. Now I'm happier. You are one hot looking stud. I thought that earlier today, and now I'll get to see all of it, not just your dick! Got to admit that when Todd came into the restroom and then made me leave, I was pretty well pissed, but now it's turning out OK, in fact – it's gonna be better than OK!"

"Well, I never got to see, up real close, just what you're carrying in your pants, like I really wanted to, so now I'll not only get to see it good and close, but I'll get to taste it too! Come on guys, let's head for Indy and really get to know each other better, OK?"

Then looking at Brian, John asked. "Guess maybe you've never had your dick stuck up in that tight ass of his yet, have you?"

"No, I sure haven't. Until just a little while ago, I didn't even know I could ask him if he'd let me do it! He told me you rammed it for a quickie today. Like it?"

"Oh yeah man, oh yeah! Slammed my rod up in that tight little hole and he made me cum like a fucking grisly bear. I'm anxious to get back at it again. Trust me man, you'll like it, you'll like it! Hey, I'm getting way too horny. You guys ready? Let's get to the motel, I need some ass!"

After John gave Todd the motel address and managed to do a quick grab and feel of both Todd's crotch and also Brian's crotch, he told Todd to just pull around to the back of the motel, park in the back lot and he'd meet them there just as soon as he got checked in and found out exactly which room number they had.

Just about an hour later, the two trucks pulled into the motel parking lot, made sure the back doors on each of the trucks were securely locked, John got checked in, and the three men were finally in a room of total privacy.

"Oh shit man, I've been wanting this ever since the little session in the restroom earlier. Come here Brian, drop 'em and let me suck on that stick for just a minute. Let's all do some initial funning around with each other for about 10 or 15 minutes, then go grab some supper up at the restaurant and then get back here, and spend the rest of the night doing the good fucking and sucking things! I haven't been in bed with two guys, at the same time for way too long now, and I'm gonna enjoy this!"

"Hey man, I want in on this!" Todd added as he watched Brian slide his pants down and John squat on the floor, putting his mouth right at crotch level. "John, take your pants off so I can get under your crotch and suck on you while you're sucking on Brian."

"Oh, hey yeah!" John enthusiastically stated. "Oh shit man, yeah! Yeah that sounds hot! Suck me hard man, suck on my dick! Oh yeah man! Oh yeah man! Oh, you suck so much better than my wife does – yeah suck me man, suck me! Suck me hard! Come on men, let's do some fast sucking, and then grab us a fast bite of supper. I wanna get back here and use both of you guys like I ain't used two guys, for a hell of a long time! Yeah, I need this!"

CHAPTER TWELVE:

Depends on the Sausage

Supper time allowed the three horny men, horny, but still trying to act very polite and not out of proper character – they forced themselves into mostly conversation of the, 'out in public' type. Todd and Brian did find out that John was the owner of a very small trucking company, and his load of carpeting, was not for his carpet business, but rather a customer's company. Much more to their specific interest, they did find out that he also owned a very small weight room that was much more of the types that used to be in existence before the large health clubs rather took over the 'lifting' business. He told Todd and Brian that it was small, did not make any money, but sure did give him the freedom and reasons for getting out of the house, for valid reasons, once in awhile. He then smiled and said, "If you understand the 'valid reasons' concept!"

Todd and Brian looked at each other, grinned, then looked back at John, grinned, and each man uttered, "Yeah, yeah, got ya! Got, ya!"

John then looked at each of the two and asked, "No wife?"

Each of the two shook their heads, "No" as John then leaned over close and quietly stated, "I think every guy should be made to do gay sex at least twice, before he is allowed to get married, just to be sure he still wants to! Would have been a good rule for me!"

One quick supper later, the men were back in their room, and laughing about how careful they had to be, in the restaurant, about not letting other customers or some of the waitresses hear some of their conversation.

As they were now rather quickly undressing and admiring each other's bodies, Brian leaned over and ran his tongue the complete length of Todd's back, all the way from his butt crack, up the middle of his back, and to the back of his neck

Todd asked, "John, you never got to finish that little story you were trying to tell us over there in the restaurant about you and that grocery store guy that you made it with last week."

"Oh yeah! Yeah, that older couple that sat down right behind us kind of stopped that one didn't it?" John smilingly replied. "Well, like I did tell you – I was in the grocery store last week-end and was standing there looking at the label on a jar of spaghetti sauce. This grocery store guy was squatted there on the floor kind of close to where I was, and he was stocking some spaghetti stuff. Anyway, I looked over toward him, guess I must have had this feeling I was being looked at, or something, and when I looked at him, he was staring right at my crotch. And I do mean, strongly enough that it made me look down to see if something was wrong or not. Nothing looked wrong, so I looked back at him again, and all of a sudden he realized that I saw him looking at my crotch."

"Were you showing something? Did you have a hardon or something?" Brian inquisitively asked!

"No, really I didn't, but I also didn't have any briefs on either, and yeah, I do admit it was hanging down my leg. So anyway, when he realized he had been staring at it and that I had seen him looking, he just kind of quickly tried to look the other way. Well, being in kind of a joking mood, I guess, I asked him, 'Oh hey guy, where can I find the polish sausage?'"

Laughing quite strongly, both Todd and Brian each, let out a quick, "Oh shit!"

"I thought that kid, well anyway I call him a kid, was gonna fall over backwards when I asked him that! His face turned beat red, and that turned me on! Again, I know he did not intend to do it, but again he looked at my crotch! Well, guys, gotta admit that with that happening, now my dick was starting to squirm in there some. He saw it! He knew I was getting horny, and I know he was too! Absent mindedly, he licked his lips. Then he realized just what in the hell he had just done. Then, again in my joking mood, I held the spaghetti sauce down toward him and asked, "Hey, is this the right kind of sauce to put on some 'seggitties' and some sausage?"

"Oh shit man, you didn't!? Oh God John, that poor guy! What in the hell did he say? What did he do?" Todd anxiously asked.

"Very calmly and very politely, he looked right at my crotch, slightly slid his tongue out some, and just said, 'Depends on the sausage!' Then looked up at me and quietly said, 'I get off at nine.' I then quietly answered, so that means I'll get off at nine-ten, right?" Looking around to make sure nobody else was getting close, he looked right back at my crotch, which by this time was starting to look like a sausage, again slightly slid his tongue out some, and just said, 'Depends on the sausage, man, depends on the sausage!'"

As John, Todd and Brian continued to undress and assemble in the queen sized bed, Brian grabbed John's dick and asked, "This sausage man, this sausage?"

"Yeah that sausage! I looked down at him – remember he's squatted down on the floor with his face right at crotch level and I just said, "We'll try this one as I tapped my dick a little, and then said, "Nine o'clock at the telephone booth. Don't be late!'"

"Oh shit man, really? Really did you guys meet?"

"Hell yeah man, hell yeah! And to just make things fun, I did go buy a polish sausage, you know those hard sausages, I think they're called Polish sausage, anyway the ones that are about 15 inches long and something that I know a lot of guys would love to feel going up their butt – well I had that with me. When he came out of the store right after nine, I just handed him the sausage. He grinned real big and just said, 'This is the wrong sausage, but thanks anyway – I want the other one!'"

"Oh shit man, oh shit! Oh God John, you have got me so fucking turned on here, telling me about you and that guy, while I'm getting to lay here and feel this sausage of yours, what in the hell did you guys do then?"

"Shit man, hey – Todd, feel this dick! Yeah, yeah, oh yeah – yeah man, this is getting so fucking hot! Hey, somebody grab my ass, but John I've gotta hear what in the hell happened with you and this guy. Was he hot? Was he built?"

"Oh shit yeah! I will admit I did not know that until I finally got his clothes off since he likes to wear those baggy loose fitting pants and his shirt was pretty loose too, but shit yeah – the body of a God once I got him stripped down. Told me his name was Jimmy, but everybody called him "Shorty", he was 20, a former gymnast in high school, and still worked out a lot and was still kind of involved in gymnastics, some. He was not particularly short, stood about five ten or so, so I'm not too sure just how everybody understood the nickname! Yeah, the boys in the locker room, that I understood, but how did everybody else know about his dick?"

"So God man, I'm sure you guys didn't do it right there in front of the store, where'd you guys go?" Todd inquired.

"Well, I asked him if he had a place we could go to, and he told me he was living with his older brother and his wife, so no, he didn't. I told him I had a wife at home, so we sure couldn't go there, but that if we killed just a few minutes, the guy running the gym that I own, would be gone, and we could go there and just leave the lights off so it didn't look to anyone like it was open. So we did. We kind of killed about 10 or 15 minutes, then he followed me to the back door of the gym."

"Oh shit man, I can not believe this! Now I really do know why you have that gym. It's your secret little sex hideout, isn't it?" Todd laughed and asked!

"Yeah I guess that's what you could call it! Well—anyway, sure does come in handy once in awhile! Like that night! Shit man, I'm sure glad I went to the grocery store that night. Little did I know that when I asked him if he knew where I could find the polish sausage, that all he needed to do was grab his crotch. Now I know why the baggy pants! The dick of death! Absolutely, the dick of death! When he's got those tight gymnastic tights on, whatever they're called, he has to show the basket of glory! God that guy is hung! I have not measured it yet, but he told me, hard, it's like ten or ten and a half. And I am damn sure it is!"

"Hey wait here – wait!" Todd jumped in! "Uhhh – you said, have not measured it yet! Meaning? I assume that means you and he are gonna do it again? Is that right!?

"Hell yeah! He got a free membership to the gym that night! Hell yeah, he gets to use the gym as often as he likes, just a long as he accepts my phone calls and kind of acts like my – what should we say, 'My standby and be ready, man?'"

"Oh shit man, damn! I guess he must have screwed you that night then, right?" Brian asked as he continued to play with and jerk on John's dick – continued to let Todd run two fingers up into his ass, and Todd presented his own ass, close enough to John's right hand, so that he too was getting an ass full of massaging fingers.

"Oh shit man! That is way too much to comprehend for me! I mean, yeah I can comprehend it, it's just that I guess I wish I could have gotten stuck with that big thing too!" Brian stated calmly.

"Well, tell you what young man!" John quickly responded. "Mine just might not be 10 or ten and a half, but I sure do know how to use what I've got, don't I Todd? He got it for a couple of minutes, earlier today, so he knows how fucking good it can feel up in your ass! Lay down here man and let me pound that sweet little ass of yours, and while I fuck the hell out if it back here, it looks to me like that big dick of Todd's could use some good warm sucking on, right Todd?"

"Yeah, man, yeah! This is gonna be kind of weird. I'm gonna let Brian, my co-worker, for what two years now Brian, finally get on my dick! Shit man, I wish like hell I had known this a long time ago. Brian, take my dick and suck it man, suck it. Come on, let's make up for lost time!"

Brian was on his gut, with John now making pounding, slamming, hay in his tight little ass and finally, finally, Brian had Todd's dick stuck down his throat! All he could think of as he tried and tried to take even more dick than there was to take, was, "Todd

– you think you're excited about me sucking on your dick, well man if you only know how many fucking times I wanted to just reach out, grab it, and just tell you that if you didn't want to get sucked, too fucking bad! Man, I've wanted to take this dick for way too long now! Come on man, cum in my mouth! Fill me with your juice man, fill me! Make my day happy, make my day happy!"

"Oh God yes Brian, yeah man – suck me man – suck me! Oh shit I can not believe how fucking long I have wanted you on my dick! Shit man, if I'd been playing around a lot longer than I have, I know damn well I would have forced you to suck me! Oh shit man, I wish we had been doing this a hell of a lot longer!"

As John was pounding Brian's ass, he asked, "So Todd, kinda guess maybe for you, it's a good thing Brian was sucking me off in the restroom, right? You never had any idea he was guy friendly?"

"I had no idea, no idea at all! Really man, of the number of times when I've kind of closed my eyes and just tried to imagine what it'd be like to have him on me, or me on him – whichever – it was just too much to imagine could ever happen! Wow! Shit yeah man! I could care less about who propositioned who! Just thank God, I walked in right then! John, just as soon as you get done in that tight little ass of his, I want that rod of yours back up in my ass! I like what's happening to Brian! He's getting his ass pounded like some swinging baseball bat, and he's getting to chew on my hungry dick like crazy. I want you pounding my ass like that, while I finally get that stick of Brian's, rammed down my throat as far as it will go!"

Brian pulled off for just a second and firmly stated, "And men, just as soon as John gets done fucking your ass, and you get done sucking on my dick, I want to fuck that ass of John's for hours and hours. God man! What a fucking good looking hairy, tight, muscled ass! God Todd, we need to double fuck him! Wanta do that?"

"Hey, yeah man, I want to do any fucking thing you two guys can think to do. Right now, I feel like I'm in heaven, maybe, 'gay heaven', and I'm getting to do anything and everything, to two guys, and with two guys, that's out of this world! Shit man! All I can say right now is, I just hope I can walk and swallow tomorrow! Up the ass, down the throat, anything and everything – let's do it! Wow, what a day! I didn't know I'd ever be so glad to catch some guy, sucking on some other guy, than I have been today! John, we don't live too far away from each other – really! We need to make sure we do this again, and real soon! You bring your buddy Shorty along, and maybe Brian can bring Shane, and wait – hey wait! Maybe I can get Scott, a hot construction guy that I know, to come and join in the fun! Hell man! I forgot! I've got me Scott that likes to play like this. He is hot, fucking, fucking, fucking – hot! Yeah men, yeah! We gotta do this! We need to get a real group orgy going! What do you guys think? Interested?"

"Interested? Hell yeah, I know I sure am!" John answered. You got another fuck buddy that you think maybe could be there? Oh shit man, gotta tell you – I've dreamed of doing something like that for a long time but never have! Yeah man, yeah! That sounds hot as hell to me! Real hot! Oh shit man, that idea is really turning me on! Let's do it!"

"Oh God Brian – I'm gonna cum man! I'm gonnnnnnnnnnna cum! Hey man – oh man – wow! Oh shit man – oh God that was hot! Oh man that felt good! God, I guess maybe the idea of getting a lot of us together must have made me hot as hell too! Brian, you OK?"

Trying to take some deep breaths, Brian attempted a quick, "Yeah, I'm OK – fucking mouth full of my buddies cum, but yeah – doing OK and feeling good!"

Pounding Brian's ass like crazy, suddenly John let out, "Brian, hang on man – I'm about to let you have it! Oh Brian – you're about to get it, you're gonna get it man, you're gonna get it – Brian here it comes man – Oh my gawd man – you're getting it in both ends man – here it comes! Oh man! Oh man! Oh my gawd Brian! Oh, your ass is so fucking hot! Shit man – Todd, you've gotta fuck this butt – you've gotta! It is so fucking hot!"

"Hey listen man! I'm gonna fuck that butt – you're gonna fuck my butt – he's gonna fuck your butt – hey every fucking and sucking thing that can happen, is gonna happen tonight, agreed!? I'm not intended on getting – any sleep tonight – none at all!"

Then looking at both Brian and John, Todd added, "All I can say right now is, 'Thank God,' for those two dildos!"

Obviously with a total look of confusion on both of there faces, Brian and John rather looked back at Todd and asked, "What!? What two dildos?"

Todd looked back at his two sex mates and said, "Men, two dildos that were my introduction to this style of living, and right then, I wasn't even using 'em! See, I was measuring a house for some carpet, and well – anyway – I'll fill you in on all the details – later – as we take our breathers, OK?"

ABOUT THE AUTHOR

Wade Wright

Wade Wright is an older gay semi-retired gentleman, who lives in Arizona, alone, except for his puppy of about 15 years. One "normal" marriage, two daughters, four grandchildren, and two sadly shortened gay partnerships, have given Wade a perspective of living very different types of lives, and uses some of those experiences, as he does his writings.

Wade Wright is also the author of ***Yes, Cops Do It – Oh Yeah, Apartment 117, The Two Straight Guys, In Cemetery Park, Marshmallow Cream – and Hard Big Pieces of Chocolate,*** and ***Jay, Jake and Jimmy***, available from The NazcaPlainsCorp.com, Amazon.com, or your local bookstore.

"YES, COPS DO IT, — OH YEAH!"

a collection of stories by

WADE WRIGHT

A BONER BOOK

WRIGHT

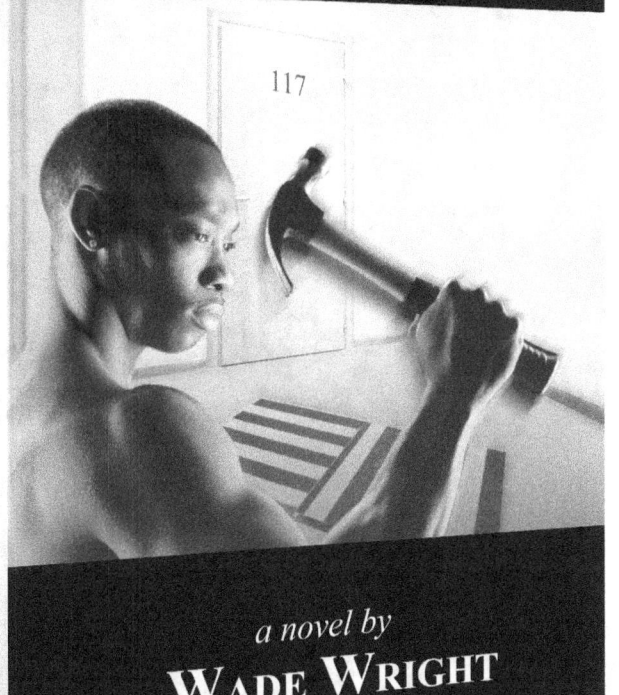

APARTMENT 117

a novel by
WADE WRIGHT

A
BONER
BOOK

WRIGHT
IN CEMETERY PARK
A BONER BOOK
IN CEMETERY PARK
A NOVEL BY
WADE WRIGHT

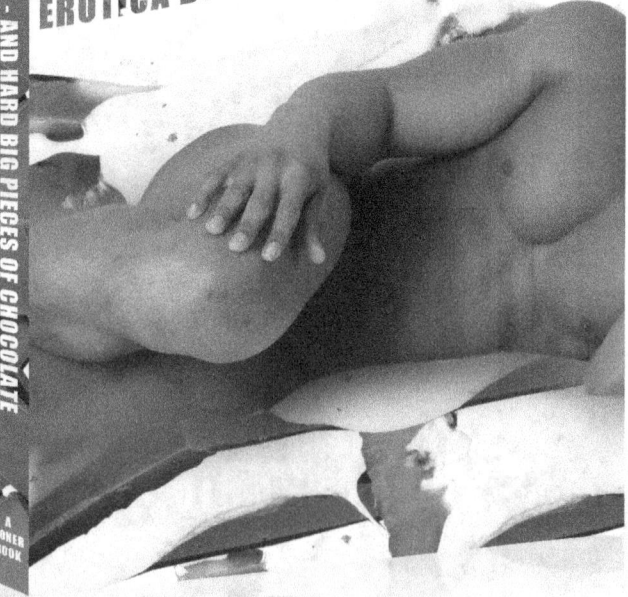

MARSHMALLOW CREAM
– AND HARD BIG PIECES OF CHOCOLATE

EROTICA BY WADE WRIGHT

A BONER BOOK

JAY, JAKE AND JIMMY

A NOVEL BY
WADE WRIGHT

WRIGHT

JAY, JAKE AND JIMMY